Amy pointed at the screen as the nurse, Lynn, resumed her checks. 'I know him.'

Lynn's eyes darted over to the television, taking in the hunk currently filling the screen. Amy bristled. She could almost hear her thoughts.

Lynn gave a small smile. 'Well, you're a lucky lady, then. I imagine he's one of the best neonatologists in the world if he's looking after the President's baby.'

'He is. I tried to get hold of him yesterday but he didn't answer the text I sent him. I guess he was busy.' The message *I need your help* had been direct and to the point without revealing anything. Her voice was quiet, thoughtful. Her hands rubbed up and down her stomach. 'How is it?' she asked as Lynn unwound the blood pressure cuff. She knew the answer before Lynn spoke, but her head was currently in another place. There was only one person in the world she trusted right now to take care of her baby. 'I can't let anything happen to this baby,' she whispered. 'He's my only chance.'

Lynn wrapped her hand around Amy's. 'I know that.' She hesitated, glancing towards the television. 'Maybe it's time to ask a friend for help?' Her eyes were fixed on the television screen. 'If I knew my baby was going to come early I'd want the finest neonatologist in the world to be at the delivery.' Her voice was firm and strong. 'Wouldn't you?'

Amy's phone beeped and she reached into her pocket. It was a reply from Linc. Three words. *Anything. Any time.*

Their eyes met. Amy bit her lip and took a deep breath. The shine of unshed tears was visible in her eyes. 'Exactly how far away is Pelican Cove?'

Dear Reader

This is my second story in the fictional setting of Pelican Cove based around the White House medical staff.

Picking a setting for a story is always difficult. When I started to write these stories I could see Pelican Cove very clearly in my head. A small town, sort of based on *Murder She Wrote*'s Cabot Cove, but set on the Californian coast. I also found a picture of a beautiful studio flat in San Francisco and used that as the setting for Lincoln's apartment. I almost wish I could have stayed there myself!

Part of this story is about a young woman who has had breast cancer. I took this part of the book very seriously, and spoke to a number of women who have beaten this disease. I hope I've captured realistically everything that they told me. The most poignant part for me is the scene in front of the mirror with Amy and Lincoln. I just hope I've done it justice.

I love to hear from readers, so please come and visit me at: www.scarlet-wilson.com

Many thanks

Scarlet

WEST WING TO MATERNITY WING!

BY
SCARLET WILSON

First published in Great Britain 2012
by Mills & Boon, an imprint of Harlequin (UK) Limited.
Harlequin (UK) Limited, Eton House, 18-24 Paradise Road,
Richmond, Surrey TW9 1SR

© Scarlet Wilson 2012

ISBN: 978 0 263 22728 4

Harlequin (UK) policy is to use papers that are natural, renewable and recyclable products and made from wood grown in sustainable forests. The logging and manufacturing process conform to the legal environmental regulations of the country of origin.

Printed and bound in Great Britain
by CPI Antony Rowe, Chippenham, Wiltshire

Scarlet Wilson wrote her first story aged eight and has never stopped. Her family have fond memories of 'Shirley and the Magic Purse', with its army of mice, all with names beginning with the letter 'M'. An avid reader, Scarlet started with every Enid Blyton book, moved on to the *Chalet School* series, and many years later found Mills and Boon®.

She trained and worked as a nurse and health visitor, and currently works in public health. For her, finding Medical Romances was a match made in heaven. She is delighted to find herself among the authors she has read for many years.

Scarlet lives on the West Coast of Scotland with her fiancé and their two sons.

Recent titles by the same author:

THE BOY WHO MADE THEM LOVE AGAIN
IT STARTED WITH A PREGNANCY

These books are also available in eBook format from www.millsandboon.co.uk

**Praise for
Scarlet Wilson:**

'Stirring, emotional and wonderfully absorbing,
IT STARTED WITH A PREGNANCY
is an impressive debut novel from a fabulous
new voice in category romance: Scarlet Wilson!'

This book is dedicated to my aunt—Margaret Wilson.
Not everyone is as lucky as I am to have
such a fabulous auntie. One who offers unfailing
support to her three nieces and many great-nieces
and nephews. And brings us wonderful holiday stories
of 'exploding' strawberries and cream!

And to my editor, Sally Williamson,
thank you for bringing me into the
Mills and Boon family and looking after me so well.
It's been a pleasure working with you.

And to women the world over
who've suffered from breast cancer. This one is for you.

PROLOGUE

LINCOLN ADAMS stuck his fingers into the collar around his neck and pulled—hard. The collar was at least an inch too small for him. It didn't matter that the whole ensemble was Italian made from the finest materials. The suit trousers were an inch too short and the waist was an uncomfortably snug fit. He kept his arms firmly by his sides, his hands clenched in his lap, because if he leaned forward onto the table in front of him, the jacket would stretch across his back, restricting his movements. It was bad enough having to borrow someone else's clothes, but when they were a size too small... The sooner he was out of here the better.

The White House press secretary swept across the room in a flurry of eye-catching blue silk with a tailored black jacket on top. Every pore of her skin emanated professionalism and efficiency, and she knew how to work a crowd. This was all her fault.

He gave a forced smile at David Fairgreaves, who sat down next to him. The old man didn't look in the least fazed by the pandemonium surrounding him. In fact, he looked as if he might actually be enjoying it. Was he mad? Then again, for an international-award-winning doctor, this would be all in a day's work.

Diane Green stood behind the podium next to him. Almost instantaneously the cameras started snapping around them and the noise level increased frenetically. She raised her hand and the press pack heeded. She had the information they'd all been waiting for.

'Thank you for joining us here today at Pelican Cove for our happy announcement. You will all be aware that President Taylor and his wife, Jennifer, were expecting their first baby on seventeenth October. However, today, on the twenty-third of August, Charles and Jennifer Taylor are delighted to announce the arrival of...' she paused for effect '...the First Daughter, Esther Rose Taylor, weighing four pounds ten ounces.'

The room around her erupted, questions being shouted from every angle. 'Isn't the baby too early?'

'What was the First Lady doing in Pelican Cove?'

'Where is her own obstetrician, Dr Blair?'

'Was the President here?'

'Where did the name come from?'

But Diane Green was the epitome of calm. Continuing with her carefully prepared statement, she lifted her hand again until the room was silent. 'Esther Rose Taylor was born at thirty-two weeks gestation. The First Lady had been ordered to rest in the last few weeks of her pregnancy and had come to Pelican Cove to do exactly that. She was accompanied by her obstetrician, Dr Blair, who unfortunately had a myocardial infarction in the last few days. As a result of that the First Lady was looked after by...' Diane Green gestured towards the seats to her right '...Dr David Fairgreaves, one of the foremost leading obstetricians in America, and Dr Lincoln Adams, one of our finest neonatologists.' She gave a little nod towards the reporters. 'I am pleased to report that the President was here for the arrival of his daughter and she is named after Jennifer Taylor's beloved and much-missed grandmother. Any questions regarding the health of the First Lady and the First Daughter—' a genuine smile swept across Diane Green's lips, as if she was still to get used to saying that '—can be answered by our two highly qualified doctors here.'

Once again the room erupted and Lincoln Adams took a deep breath as this time the barrage of questions was directed at him. *Let me out of here!*

Amy Carson sat on the cold, clinical hospital bed, usually occupied by a patient, her hands fixed firmly on her swollen stomach. The plaster was falling off the ceiling above her and the wall hadn't seen a coat of paint in— How long? What did the patients who usually ended up in this room think? The role reversal of staff member to potential patient wasn't lost on her. Everything about this place was bland. Did she really want to end up delivering her baby in a place like this?

She gulped. How had she ended up here? The door opened and the nurse appeared again, wheeling the trolley that held the foetal monitor and sphygmomanometer. Amy felt herself tense. She knew it was going to be the same again—borderline.

She loved her colleagues here, but none of them had the specialist skills and expertise that this baby would need. More than that—nowhere in the surrounding area had facilities to deal with a premature baby. Everything about this made her uncomfortable. If only Lincoln would answer his phone...

Movement on the television in the corner of the room caught her eye. She leaned forward. 'Can you turn that up, please, Lynn?'

Her colleague nodded and automatically twisted the knob on the antiquated television set. 'Delighted to announce the arrival of...'

Amy listened to the announcement. Another baby born too early. But probably the most famous baby in the world. A baby that would have the most prestigious, experienced medical care that money could buy.

No! Surely not? Amy's chin dropped to her chest. Lincoln Adams. *Her Lincoln Adams* was shifting uncomfortably on the screen in front of her. He tugged at his shirt and answered question after question about the baby's condition. His voice was rich, smooth. If she couldn't see his image on the television in front of her, she'd imagine he was the calmest man in the world. But he wasn't. And she could tell he hated every moment of this.

Delivering the President's baby. Wow. So that's where he'd been.

Her heart constricted in her chest. Six years and he still had the same effect on her—even in her current state. She watched as he took a question from a blonde journalist, dazzling her with his twinkling blue eyes and easy smile. He was still a flirt. It was so ingrained in him that he didn't even realise he was doing it. One smile from Linc and the journalist, covering the biggest story of her life, was a babbling mess.

She pointed at the screen as the nurse, Lynn, resumed her checks. 'I know him.'

Lynn's eyes darted over to the screen, taking in the hunk currently filling the screen. Amy bristled. She could almost hear her thoughts.

Lynn gave a small smile. 'Well, you're a lucky lady, then. I imagine he's one of the best neonatologists in the world if he's looking after the President's baby.'

'He is. I tried to get hold of him yesterday but he didn't answer the text I sent him. I guess he was busy.' The message "*I need your help*" had been direct and to the point without revealing anything. Her voice was quiet, thoughtful. Her hands rubbing up and down her stomach. 'How is it?' she asked as Lynn unwound the blood-pressure cuff. She knew the answer before Lynn spoke but her head was currently in another place. There was only one person in the world she trusted right now to take care of her baby.

Lynn frowned. 'Actually, it's a little higher. I'm sorry, Amy, but as a fellow professional I'm not going to beat around the bush. With your other symptoms, it's definitely looking like borderline pre-eclampsia. The good thing is we've caught it early. It's time to see your obstetrician. And from one colleague to another, I definitely think it's time to stop work.'

Amy nodded her head, tears prickling at the sides of her eyes as she swallowed the lump in her throat. 'I can't let anything happen to this baby,' she whispered. 'He's my only chance.'

Lynn wrapped her hand around Amy's. 'I know that.' She hesitated, glancing towards the television. 'Maybe it's time to ask a friend for help?' Lynn's eyes fixed on the television screen. 'If I knew my baby was going to come early I'd want the finest neonatologist in the world to be at the delivery.' Her voice was firm and strong. 'Wouldn't you?'

Her phone beeped and she reached into her pocket. Two words. Anything. Any time.

Their eyes met. Amy bit her lip and took a deep breath, the shine of unshed tears visible in her eyes. 'Exactly how far away is Pelican Cove?'

CHAPTER ONE

LINCOLN burst through the doors to the adjoining office and wrenched the scarlet tie from his throat. The force popped the button on his shirt and sent it flying across the floor.

David Fairgreaves strolled in behind him and lifted one grey eyebrow. He took off his suit jacket, hanging it on the chair behind him. 'Problem, Lincoln?' He looked vaguely amused, another irritation to add to Lincoln's list.

Lincoln stalked over to a nearby shelf and pulled down a pair of green scrubs—he wasn't wearing this damn too-tight suit a second longer.

Washington's finest shirt lay in a crumpled heap at his feet as he pulled the scrub top over his head and turned to face David. 'How can they ask questions like that?'

David gave a little shrug of his shoulders, picked up an apple from the nearby table and crunched into it, putting his feet up on the desk. 'They're animals.'

Lincoln shook his head. 'How can you stand it? How can you sit there and smile at those idiots?'

'You've got to give it some perspective. I've just looked after the First Lady. It's news that they'll report all around the world. And they'll all be looking for their own spin— their own edge to make them stand out from the pack. Truth be known—I really don't care what any of them think. The only thing I care about is my patient.'

Lincoln stared at him. David was the only reason he'd come here in the first place. The chance to work with the man who'd been the first to retrieve stem cells was too good an opportunity to miss. The irony of it was—he looked like a bumbling old fool but was probably the most forward-thinking clinician Lincoln had ever met.

David caught him with his sharp gaze. 'What's with you anyway? You've been like a bear with a sore head all afternoon.'

Linc sighed. The man missed nothing. 'I got a strange text message last night from someone I haven't seen in years—at least, I think that's who it was from. I've texted back but I can't seem to get a signal right now, so I don't know if she's replied.' He held his cellphone up near the window and turned in various directions. Still no signal.

David gave him a knowing look. 'I take it this was a female someone?'

Linc nodded and smiled. 'Let's just say it was an unexpected blast from the past.'

'A good one?'

'She certainly wasn't that easy to forget so I hope so. But with everything that's happened in the last two days I've just not had a minute.' He ran his fingers through his dark brown hair. 'I can't remember the last time I actually slept.'

David nodded. 'Having the head of White House Security turn up at your door at three in the morning and tell you to pack up to deliver the President's baby would flatten most men.' He frowned. 'Your text. Was it from a real friend? Or a fair-weather friend? I've experienced lots of those—people who the minute you appear in the media have apparently been your "best friend" or "closest colleague" for years—even though they don't know when your birthday is or what car you drive. Fame does funny things to folks—you need to be careful, Lincoln. This is a whole new ball game for you.'

Lincoln looked thoughtful. He gestured towards the door. 'Well, that was my first official television appearance, so she can't have known anything about it. She sounded—I don't know—in trouble.'

'Just what every man loves—a damsel in distress.' David flashed him a smile. 'Come on, Lincoln, let's go and look after our girls.' He tossed his apple core into a trash can on the other side of the room.

'I told you to stop calling me that. It's Linc. My friends call me Linc.'

David looked aghast. 'Linc? Certainly not. You, my friend, are named after the finest President we've ever had and you should wear that name with pride.' He put his hand on the doorhandle as a frown puckered his forehead. 'Just don't tell Charlie Taylor I said that.'

Lincoln laughed. 'I may well use that as blackmail material.'

Amy glanced at her watch as the cab seemed to meander up the coastal road. The traffic was almost at a standstill and she watched as only a few vehicles got through the cordon in front of them. The rest were directed to turn and head back down the hill. Her stomach churned. This had to be the worst idea she'd ever had.

A uniformed officer approached the cab and rapped sharply on the window. He glanced in the back seat towards Amy. 'Where are you headed?'

The taxi driver gestured behind him. 'Got a pregnant lady to drop at the hospital.'

The cop gave a little start. He looked like a man who had heard every line in the book today but he leaned forward a little to get a better look. He obviously hadn't heard this one yet. 'Can you step out the car please, ma'am?'

Amy fumbled for the doorhandle and stepped out into the warm sea air. She pulled some money from her purse and handed it to the driver. 'Thanks very much.'

The cop ran his eyes up and down the length of her body. It was almost as if he was checking she actually *was* pregnant. Her white tunic and expanding trousers flapped in the wind, exposing every part of her body, including the currently out-turned umbilicus. She pressed her hands self-consciously over her stomach.

'Your name, ma'am?'

'Excuse me?'

'You have to give me your name—and the name of the doctor you have an appointment to see.'

Amy hesitated. 'I don't exactly have an appointment, but I'm here to see Dr Lincoln Adams.'

The cop looked down at the list in his hand and stared at her. 'This isn't exactly the time for social calls.' His eyes narrowed suspiciously, 'Dr Adams, he's a neonatologist, isn't he?' He nodded towards her stomach. 'What do you want to see him for? You haven't had your baby yet—shouldn't you be seeing an obstetrician?'

Amy sighed. The sun in Mendocino Valley was strong. She could feel it beating down on the pale skin at the parting in her red hair. A parting she usually always kept covered—too bad she'd forgotten her sunhat. She swallowed nervously. Trust her to get the cop who was smarter than the average bear.

She fumbled around her bag, looking for the bottle of water she had been drinking in the cab. Two hours in a cab with no air-conditioning with the heat so strong you could practically see it rising from the ground. Four hours in a train beforehand that had been packed with tourists. This trip had been a nightmare. There was no way she wasn't getting to see Lincoln.

She pulled her tunic from her sweating back. At least the sea winds around her were giving some relief.

'Ma'am?'

The cop was getting annoyed. She could sense that good cop had retreated and bad cop was hovering near the door.

'Here.' She pulled out a battered envelope from her bag containing her medical notes. 'Give these to Lincoln Adams, he'll see me.'

The cop rolled his eyes. 'Dr Adams is currently looking after the First Daughter. He won't see you or anyone else.' He pointed in the direction of a cluster of reporters as he handed the notes back to her. 'Nice try, though.'

Amy felt a wave of panic wash over her as her baby gave a few anxious kicks. This heat was really starting to get to her. What if Lincoln wouldn't see her? What if he refused to look after her baby when it was born? What if didn't even *remember* her?

The blood rushed to her cheeks. Surely he hadn't forgotten her? How could he possibly forget those six months spent on the Amazon aid boat? She couldn't forget a single minute. The hours they hadn't spent working, they'd spent in his bed—and neither of them had been sleeping.

Trouble was, even though she remembered every minute of their time together, did he? She'd heard sneaky rumours that Lincoln had had a long line of female friends on his Amazon trips. Was it possible she had been just another pretty face to him? Had she just been a summer-long fling?

Six months with the most gorgeous man on earth. A man who hadn't cared about appearances. He hadn't been looking for a designer-clothed, styled woman, piled with make-up. Which was just as well since her luggage had gone astray at Iquitos airport in Peru and hadn't arrived until two weeks later. She'd spent the first two weeks with her hair pulled back in her solitary hair bobble, wearing pale blue or green surgical scrubs and paper knickers. Just as well her breasts hadn't been big enough to really need the support of a bra.

She looked downwards. Things had certainly changed in the last six years. In more ways than one. Her extended stomach was definitely evidence of that.

Her hands went back to guarding her stomach. Her precious bundle. Her one and only chance of motherhood. Was it so wrong to want the best man in the land to look after her baby? More than that, someone she trusted. Someone she'd seen battle the odds to help a baby survive. Someone who refused to take no for an answer.

She wanted that. She wanted that for her baby—her son. Lincoln was the best neonatologist she'd ever worked with. If anyone could help her with an early delivery, it was him.

Her eyes drifted upwards. The cop was dealing with someone else now and looking more and more agitated by the minute. The sun was obviously getting to him too.

She looked around her. Security was everywhere. And no wonder. If reports were to be believed, the President, the First Lady and the First Daughter were currently in the hospital at the top of the hill. So how was she going to get in there?

Amy took a deep breath. 'Officer, officer!'

The cop scowled at her and walked back along the cordon. 'You again. What do you want?'

'You never let me finish,' she panted as she pushed her stomach out as far as she could. 'Lincoln Adams—he's my husband. So you have to let me in to see him.'

Where had that come from?

Amy was starting to feel light-headed. She really needed

a seat. Oh, boy. She was definitely going to be caught out now. The cop squinted at her, 'You do know I'll radio up and check, don't you?' It was almost as if he could read her panicking mind and was giving her a last-minute opportunity to give up the madness, admit that she'd lied and retreat—never to be seen again.

But Amy was determined. She would see Lincoln, no matter what. She would get him to look after her son, no matter what. She drew herself up to her whole five feet five inches and stared him straight in the eye. 'Can you tell Dr Adams that his wife, Amy Carson, is here?'

'Different names, huh?' The cop eyed her suspiciously as he lifted his shoulder to speak into the radio attached to the front of his protective vest.

Amy's hands rested on the steel grating in front of her. Her eyes drifted across the nearby ocean. It was beautiful here. But the Californian heat seemed to be suffocating her. She could feel the sun beating down, making her itchy and scratchy. In fact, her whole body felt itchy. She pulled her smock top away from her body in an attempt to get some air circulating.

She blinked. A wave of nausea swept over her. Her head was beginning to spin. Suddenly watching the boats bobbing up and down in the cove didn't seem like such a good idea. The momentum of the waves was making her feel worse, her legs turning to jelly, and little patches of black had appeared at the edge of her vision…

'Ma'am! Ma'am, are you okay? Quick! Someone get me an ambulance!

'Dr Adams!'

The voice cut across the emergency department like a siren. Lincoln spluttered his coffee all down the front of his scrubs and onto his open white coat. He glanced at the cup of lukewarm coffee. His first since yesterday and he wasn't going to get to drink it. He tossed the cup in the trash and turned towards the voice.

James Turner. Head of the President's security detail. Not again. This man was beginning to haunt his dreams—both at night and during the day.

But something was wrong. He had someone—a woman—in his arms. Linc strode towards him as James Turner unceremoniously dumped the woman on top of a gurney behind one of the sets of curtains. Beads of sweat dripped down his forehead and nose. Linc wondered if he'd managed to change out of his obligatory black suit at all since he'd arrived in Pelican Cove.

'I think I found something belonging to you, Dr Adams.'

'To me? I don't think so.' Lincoln shook his head and moved over to the gurney.

'Really?' James Turner raised an eyebrow. 'You mean you don't recognise your own wife?'

'My what?'

'I knew it. Another scam artist. It's ridiculous the lengths some of these reporters will go to. Don't worry, I'll get rid of her.'

Linc moved nearer the woman on the gurney. Her head and body were turned away from him but from the back the curly red hair looked like someone else's. Someone he'd known five years ago. Only then she'd spent most of the time with it tied up in a ponytail, not spread across her shoulders and back, like it was now.

He leaned closer, then started. Yip. That definitely was a very pregnant abdomen. At least six months. His eyes flickered to her face. Pale skin, flawless, almost translucent, with a faint sprinkling of freckles across her nose. And she was out cold. And James Turner was trying to pull her upwards, obviously thinking she was faking.

'Stop!'

This time his voice was every bit as loud as James's had been.

The cold, hard stare he was getting used to met him again.

'Get your hands off her.' Lincoln walked around to the other side of the gurney. He had to be sure. He had to be sure his eyes were not deceiving him.

No. They weren't. This was Amy Carson. This was *his* Amy Carson. The one he'd spent six hot, sweaty months with on the Amazon aid boat. Spending the days looking after a range of newborn ailments and spending the nights lost in the sea of her red hair. And he could absolutely authenticate it was her natural colour. This was definitely Amy Carson. The same one that had asked for help only forty-eight hours ago.

A very pregnant Amy Carson.

'What happened?' he asked James, as he spotted the crumpled envelope at the top of her bag. No one usually carried an envelope that size—not unless they were carrying their hospital notes.

'I got radioed from the checkpoint. She was apparently making a scene, saying she had to see you. The cop on duty had her sussed the moment he saw her. The paparazzi have been trying every angle to get up here. Never thought they would resort to this, though. It's really taking it a bit too far. She collapsed down at the checkpoint a few minutes ago.'

Lincoln stuck his head from behind the curtain. 'Nancy, I need some help in here. Can you get me a foetal monitor, please?' he shouted to one of the E.R. nurses. He turned back angrily to James, 'And you? Go and get David Fairgreaves and tell him I need him to see a patient.' He yanked the cardiac monitor leads and BP cuff from the wall. 'Not every person you meet is trying to get to the President, Mr Turner.' He touched the pale face lying on the gurney. 'She—' his voice lowered automatically '—was trying to get to me.'

He waited for James to depart and pulled the curtain tightly closed.

Amy Carson.

The girl he'd searched for. The only girl to ever get under his guard. He'd almost resigned himself to the fact he wasn't going to see her again. But here she was, in the flesh, right before his eyes again. Except her flesh had expanded considerably, creating a nice neat bump under her breasts. Nothing like how she'd looked the last night he'd seen her as she'd danced about their cabin in her underwear, laughing and teasing him. This time she wasn't laughing at all, she was out cold. And she'd been looking for him. What on earth was going on?

Nancy came in, clutching the Doppler scanner, and grabbed a nearby patient gown. She pushed Lincoln aside as he struggled with Amy's long white smock top. 'Here, let me,' she said, as she deftly manoeuvred the top out of place, replacing it with a Velcro-fastened green gown. Her hand slid underneath the gown as she attached the leads from the cardiac monitor and pressed the button to switch the machine on. Lincoln fixed the cuff on Amy's arm and watched for a few seconds as it inflated. Without saying a word, he already knew what it would say.

Nancy pulled a white plastic patient clothing bag from the locker and folded Amy's white smock. Her eyes fell on the patient notes, still in their battered envelope, currently lying at the bottom of the bed. 'Have you read those yet?'

'No. I haven't had a chance. Why?'

'Do you know her?'

He hesitated. But Nancy was as sharp as a tack. 'Do you want me to get someone else to see her?'

Linc shook his head. 'I asked James Turner to go find David Fairgreaves for me.' He waved his hand over Amy's stomach. 'I'm not an obstetrician.'

Nancy picked up the notes beside the bed and started to write down her heart rate and BP. 'I need a name, Linc.'

Lincoln picked up the Doppler scanner and put a little gel on Amy's stomach. He pulled her maternity trousers down slightly, adjusting them to reach the area that he needed to. He slid the transducer across her abdomen and after a few seconds he heard it. There. Thump, thump, thump. Like a little butterfly beating its wings. The baby's heartbeat. Whatever had happened to Amy, her baby was safe. A smile broke out across his face.

'Linc, I need a name—for the admission notes?'

'It's Amy. Amy Carson.'

'Do you know her date of birth?'

He blinked. 'August 14.'

Then he realised something. He picked up the buff-coloured folder from the bottom of the gurney. 'You could have got all that from the notes she brought with her.'

Nancy smiled. 'Yes, I could have. But the fact you know it makes it all the more interesting why this young lady ran the gauntlet today to see you. Pelican Cove just got a whole lot more interesting. Something you want to tell me, Dr Adams?' Her eyes were fixed expectantly on Amy's stomach—as if Lincoln had a closely guarded secret to tell. She leaned over and stuck the tympanic thermometer in Amy's ear.

He shook his head firmly and let out an almost forced laugh. 'You can't possibly think...'

Nancy rolled her eyes. 'I never said a word.' She picked up the notes. 'I'll go and get Ms Carson logged into the system...' her eyes swept over the nearby locker '...and bring her some water. I think she'll need it. This girl's overheated. I wonder how long she was standing out in the sun.'

Lincoln watched as she swept out of the cubicle. His eyes drifted back to the monitor.

Amy's heart rate was slow and steady but her BP...? It was way too high. He glanced at the chart. Her temperature was above normal too. He pulled up a nearby chair and sat down next to her. The noise of the E.R. seemed to fade away.

It was the first time he'd seen her in six years. His Amazonian fling. One of the best things that had ever happened to him. Six months of hard work and great sex. She'd left to go back to the US for a holiday but had told him she would be coming back in a few weeks to rejoin the boat. Next thing he knew, two weeks had passed and she'd quit. With no reason. And no forwarding address.

So what had happened to her? What had she been doing for the last six years? And why had she texted him two days ago, asking for help? Was it about this? About being pregnant?

Because this was last thing he'd been expecting.

Over the last few years he'd tried to push Amy completely from his mind. And if thoughts of her ever did creep in, they certainly didn't look like this! He'd always imagined he might meet her again on another aid boat or working in a different hospital. He certainly hadn't expected her to seek him out as a patient. And it made him almost resentful. A sensation he hadn't expected.

He reached out and touched her skin again. She was hot. She hadn't had a chance to cool back down in the air-conditioned E.R. One of her red curls was stuck to her forehead and his fingers swept across her skin to pull it back.

She murmured. Or groaned. He wasn't sure which. His hand cupped her cheek for a second. Just like he used to. And her head flinched. Moved closer. As if his hand and her cheek were a good fit. As if they were where they were supposed to be.

Something stirred inside him. And he shifted uncomfortably. They hadn't made each other any promises. He'd been surprised that she hadn't come back—had been surprised that she hadn't got in touch. She'd had his mobile number, scribbled on a bit of paper, but he hadn't had hers. She hadn't brought her phone to the Amazon with her, thinking it would never work there. And she couldn't remember her number. But it hadn't mattered, because he'd thought he would be seeing her again in two weeks.

Only he hadn't. Not until now.

That was the trouble of having a reputation as a playboy—sooner or later you started believing your own press. Everyone had expected him just to take up with the next pretty nurse that crossed his path—so had he. But something had been wrong. That pale-skinned redhead hadn't been so easy to forget. Amy Carson had got under his skin.

Even two years later, when he'd found himself swept along into an engagement with an elegant brunette, something just hadn't felt right. The first whiff of wedding plans had made him run for the hills. And he hadn't stopped. Until now.

His eyes darted to her notes and he picked them up, flicking them between his fingers. He wasn't her obstetrician, he shouldn't really read them. But he had acted as an E.R. admitting doctor, so surely that meant he should find out about his patient's history?

But he couldn't. He couldn't do that. There was a boundary here. David Fairgreaves was much more qualified to look after her and he would be here in a matter of minutes. There were some ethical lines that he wasn't sure he wanted to cross.

He looked at her overstuffed black shoulder bag. Maybe he should look in there? Maybe she might have her mobile and there could be someone he could contact for her? Or what about a next of kin? She was pregnant, so there was probably a husband.

The thought stopped him dead. He stared at her left hand. It was bare. Did that mean there was no husband? So who was the baby's father?

He pulled the bag up onto his lap. For some reason it felt wrong. Awkward. To go searching through an almost stranger's bag. Years ago, as an attending doctor he would have had no qualms about this. Lots of patients came into the E.R. in an unconscious state and had their pockets or bags searched. This was something he'd done a hundred times before. So why didn't he want to do it now?

And then it happened. Her dark green eyes flickered open. And a smile spread across her face. 'Linc,' she whispered huskily, her lips dry and her throat obviously parched. 'Do you always search through your wife's handbag?'

CHAPTER TWO

HE STARTED. For a second he'd been lost in his own thoughts. He should have known better. That was what you always got from Amy. *Miss Unpredictable*. That was the nickname the staff on the aid boat had given her. She'd never said what you expected her to say. Maybe that was what made her so unforgettable.

Everything about her was the same. And yet, everything about her was different. She gave a little smile as she tried to sit up on the gurney and he moved swiftly to her side to help adjust the backrest and pillows, automatically pressing the button for the electronic BP monitor again. Her smile was disarming him. It reminded him of a hundred things that weren't appropriate for an E.R. It reminded him of a hundred things that probably weren't appropriate for a pregnant lady. He felt his breath leave his body—had he been holding it? And felt the tension leave his shoulder muscles. He could stop worrying. She was awake.

'So what's the problem, *Mrs Adams*?'

Amy's heart was fluttering in her chest and she didn't know if it was to do with her medical condition or from the effect of seeing Lincoln in the flesh again. Thank goodness she was currently lying down, because she was sure her legs had just turned to mush. Old blue eyes was back.

All six feet, broad shoulders and dark curly hair of him. Hair you could just run your fingers through...

Her grin spread wider, then she laid her hand on his arm. 'I'm sorry about that, Linc. But it's like Fort Knox out there and I really needed to see you.' Her mind was spinning. Could he hear her heart beating frantically in her chest? Could he know the effect that he still had on her, six years on? She hadn't expected this. She'd expected to get in here and persuade him to look after her baby if she delivered early. Instead, she found herself being pulled into his deep blue eyes. Deeper and deeper.

'Amy, I'm happy to see you. Doubtless, I would have been happier if it was six years ago, but you didn't need to lie to get in here.'

She sat back against the pillows. 'Wow. You don't beat about the bush.'

'Neither do you apparently.' His eyes were resting on her abdomen but his voice had reverted back to teasing.

She took a deep breath. It didn't matter that something was currently doing flip-flops in her stomach. She needed to focus. To let him know how important he was to her right now. 'I did need to tell lies to get in here, Linc. It was really important that I see you and the cop had already told me to go away.'

'So you decided to faint?' He raised his eyebrow at her.

She gave a little laugh. 'Nah, the heat decided that for me.' Her eyes fixed on his and she hesitated a little. 'I did try to text you—but you weren't answering—and then I saw you on the television this morning and realised where you'd been.'

He pulled the chair back over and sat next to her again. 'Yeah, I've been kind of busy. And I should warn you—I haven't slept in two days.'

She rolled her eyes. 'Oh, no! You're like a bear with

sore head when you don't sleep. I pity the poor nursing staff working with you.'

A lazy smile crept across his face. 'You're the second person to say that to me today.'

She felt something wrench at her. It was so easy to fall back into their way of teasing each other. It was so easy to forget the most obvious reason she was here. Six years felt like nothing. It was almost as if the last time they'd spoken had been yesterday. She knew him so well. But who else knew the same things about him that she did?

She bit her lip. There was every chance that Lincoln was happily married. But she wasn't here looking for romance. She wasn't here because he was the best lover she'd ever had. This was even more personal than that. He had no idea how much life had changed for her in the last six years. She was only half the woman he used to know... She gave herself a shake. She was here to find someone she trusted to look after her baby. The most precious thing in the world to her.

He shook his head. 'Enough about me. Let's get back to the matter at hand.' His voice dipped. 'Why are you here, Amy? What do you want from me?'

The professional head was gone again. This time, the hundred questions that were spinning around his head in frustration came bubbling to the surface. He hadn't seen her in six years. She'd appeared out of the blue, pregnant and asking for him. What on earth was going on?

She touched her abdomen. 'I have signs of pre-eclampsia and this baby means more to me than anything in this world. If my baby is born prematurely I want him to have the best chance in the world.' She hesitated for a second, before looking into his eyes. 'And I knew the best chance for my baby would be you.'

Lincoln shook his head and his brow furrowed. He

waved his arm. 'You must know a dozen doctors who could take care of your baby. Why me, Amy?'

Her answer was immediate and straight to the point and he could see tears glistening in her eyes. 'I might know a dozen doctors, Linc, but none of them are like you. You're the best. The best neonatologist I've ever known. You did things on that boat that TV movies are made out of—with virtually no equipment and only the most unskilled staff.' She gestured towards herself.

He shook his head. 'You're not unskilled, Amy. You're a damn fine nurse and you know it.'

'I'm a damn fine *theatre* nurse, Linc. I had no experience at all with neonates. I went there as a specialist nurse in eye theatre, and that was fine for all the cataract, squint and glaucoma surgeries. I even managed to struggle through with cleft-palate surgeries and emergency appendectomies. But I'd never really worked as a general, medical or paediatric nurse before—I'd never looked after pregnant women before. I was seriously out of my depth and you helped me—you know you did.'

Lincoln leaned over and took her hand again. 'But we were a team, Amy, we helped each other. Everyone was selected because of their individual skills and level of expertise. But at the end of the day we treated what came through the door.'

She shook her head. 'No one was as dedicated to those babies as you were, Linc. You were the one who would stay up half the night, watching over them.' His brow furrowed. 'Why was that, Linc? I asked before, but you wouldn't tell me.'

He shrugged his shoulders and she could see him searching for the words. His eyes looked darker than normal, heavier from fatigue. He sat down next to her. 'My sister had a premature baby around twenty years ago.

There weren't any facilities near where we stayed and her daughter—my niece—died.'

Amy took a sharp breath and rested her hand on his shoulder.

He gave a rueful smile. 'My sister was ten years older than me at the time. I watched my little niece struggle for breath, turn blue and die. Our family didn't really talk about it after that. It was too painful. I hadn't really been interested in school before then. I was just coasting along. But everything changed after that. I knew if I wanted to be a doctor to help babies like my niece, I had to knuckle down and get the grades—so I did. Medicine for neonates has come a long way in the last twenty years. If my niece had been born now, she would have survived.'

'You never said anything. Why didn't you tell me this on the boat?'

Lincoln met her with a pointed stare. 'Some things are easier not to talk about—don't you think?'

The heavy air hung between them. Amy held her breath, waiting to see if he would say anything else.

'Dr Adams?'

A nurse appeared at the curtains, with David standing behind her. 'They need you in NICU.'

NICU. The neonatal intensive care unit. A place that normally didn't exist in Pelican Cove—there had never been a need for it. A place that currently held the First Daughter. In the last two days more personnel and supplies had been transferred down from San Francisco Children's Hospital than he'd thought possible. Didn't there have to be more than one baby for it to be termed an NICU? He pushed the thoughts from his mind.

'What can I do for you folks?' David strode through the curtains with his normal joie de vivre. Lincoln's eyes met his and he lifted the battered envelope from the bottom of the gurney and handed it to him. 'I need you to see a friend of mine, please, David.'

David's face changed, his eyes taking in the patient on the bed. The pregnant patient on the bed. He pulled the notes from the envelope, glancing to see which hospital they had come from, then gave Lincoln an inquisitive stare.

'My patient now, Dr Adams.' David's manner was brisk and to the point. 'I'll let you know if I need you.' His tone was almost dismissive. Whilst at times he gave the impression of being a bumbling fool, as a clinician he was second to none. And Lincoln knew it—it was why he'd asked for David's help. Amy couldn't be in safer hands. But there was no mistaking who would be in charge here.

Linc took a deep breath and stepped away from the gurney. 'I'll be back,' he muttered, his eyes not meeting hers, and he stepped through the curtains.

David's hand caught his shoulder. 'Dr Adams?'

The professional title. He must be annoyed. 'Yes?'

'Just remember your first and *only* priority is the First Daughter. Don't let other things get in the way. Don't get distracted.'

'You think I am?' The words came out automatically, snappier than he expected.

David's voice was quiet. The voice of years of learning and experience, both academically and human. 'I think you could be. Let me handle this.' He turned and ducked behind the curtains, pulling them tightly shut behind him.

Linc walked the few hundred yards along the corridor. Pelican Cove was a small community hospital, not a sprawling metropolis with new technology sprouting from every corner. That was why, when the First Lady had gone into labour here, he'd had to transfer staff and equipment from San Francisco Children's Hospital to ensure the safe delivery of the thirty-two-weeker.

As usual, the black-suited security detail was at the door—it was getting to the point they just blended into the background. He pushed open the door to the newly kitted-out NICU. The heat encompassed him immediately, the temperature warmer in here to compensate for the early arrival's rapid heat loss.

He walked over to the incubator. Two of his best nurses were on duty.

'What's up?'

For a premature baby, the First Daughter had an air of determination about her, obviously a chip off the old block. She'd come out screaming, breathing on her own and continued to do so.

He glanced at the nearby monitor. Her O2 levels were good and there was no nasal flaring.

'She's not feeding well. In fact, we can't get her to latch on at all.'

Lincoln frowned. A common complaint in premature babies who hadn't yet learned how to suck. 'What about kangaroo care?'

Ruth, the nurse, nodded and stared down at her charge, 'The only reason Esther is back in here is because Jennifer Taylor is currently sleeping. She's exhausted. Up until now it's been skin-to-skin contact the whole time. Six hours since delivery and we've not managed to get her to feed yet.' She leaned over the incubator. 'And little missy is getting cranky.'

Lincoln scrubbed his hands at the nearby sink. He'd already examined Esther just after delivery, but there was no harm in rechecking. He pulled on some sterile gloves and slid his hands into the incubator. He ran his hand around and inside her mouth, ensuring her palate was correctly formed. Checked her skin tone, colour and fontanel for clinical signs of dehydration. Sounded her chest to check her heart and lungs and gently probing her small abdomen. Once he was finished he stripped off his gloves, washed and dried his hands again and checked her charts.

'Okay, there are no immediate problems, except her blood glucose has dropped slightly since delivery. Once Jennifer Taylor wakes up, can you give me a shout and I'll go and have a chat with her? I'm really reluctant to start any kind of supplementary or tube-feeding. At thirty-two weeks I think she's more than capable of breastfeeding and I don't want to do anything that will jeopardise that. We might have to suggest that Jennifer expresses some milk in the meantime to try and get some fluid into her.'

Ruth gave a nod. 'I'm sure she'll be awake shortly. I'll give you a shout.'

Lincoln entered some notes in the electronic record and went back outside, glancing at his watch. Half an hour. Would David Fairgreaves be finished with Amy yet?

He walked over to the nurses' station, glancing around him before picking up Amy's notes. They were thicker than he would have expected for a healthy woman her age and he started to flick through them to read over her obstetric care. If he was going to look after her baby he needed to know what he was dealing with. *IVF pregnancy.* The words caught his attention instantly.

Why had Amy needed IVF? His fingers went backwards through the notes—away from the area of his expertise—and froze at the long clinical letter near the end. His eyes scanned it quickly, his breath catching in his throat. The diagnosis was in bold type at the head of the letter. Breast cancer. Amy had breast cancer.

No. She was too young. She didn't smoke, rarely drank alcohol, and lived a relatively healthy lifestyle. How on earth could she be a candidate for breast cancer? It seemed unreal. Even though the words and clinical evidence were there in front of him. He couldn't believe it. It was almost as if he were reading about someone else.

His eyes raked the letter for a date. And his brain did rapid calculations. He felt himself sag into a nearby chair.

Six years ago. Her diagnosis had been made six years ago when she'd left the Amazon boat. Had she known she was sick? Why on earth hadn't she told him?

His hands skipped over her treatment plans, test results—some good, some bad. He turned to the inside cover of the notes, searching for her next of kin.

Nothing. No one listed. He'd known that her mother and father had died a few years before she'd joined the boat. She'd gone through all this herself?

Something twisted in his gut. Surprise. Anger. Hurt.

She hadn't told him—and he was hurt. Six months he'd spent with her. They might not have confessed undying love to each other, but surely she'd known he would have supported her? Wasn't that what friends did?

After all, that was why she was here now. She needed help—or her baby did. She obviously felt she could ask him for help now, so why not then?

He could feel the tension in his neck and jaw. Irrational anger built inside him. His fingers brushed the notes again. He had to push this stuff aside. He had to deal with her in a professional capacity.

He edged back along the corridor, approaching the curtains quietly. Two seconds later he heard a peal of laughter.

Not girly. Not tinkling. Deep, hearty, genuine laughter. David had obviously turned on his natural charm again. The man could have people eating out of his hand within two minutes of meeting them. Something about the ease and instant familiarity between the two of them bothered him. Made him want to march into the cubicle and stand between them. How crazy was that?

Linc cleared his throat loudly and edged his way between the curtains. 'How's things?'

David turned to face him, his head flicking back towards her. 'Amy? Are you happy for Dr Adams to know about your condition?'

Amy blinked. They obviously hadn't had that part of the conversation yet. 'Actually, Dr Fairgreaves, Lincoln's the reason I'm here. If this baby is coming early, I'm hoping that Lincoln will look after him for me.'

Lincoln cast his eyes over the monitor again, noting her rising blood pressure. 'And is it, David? Is this baby coming early?' Did he really want to have two premature babies in a community hospital not designed for the task?

David's face remained static, expressionless to the underlying current of tension between the two of them. He nodded briefly and handed the notes to Lincoln.

'Ms Adams in twenty-eight weeks pregnant. For the last few days Amy has shown some mild signs of pre-eclampsia. A slight rise in blood pressure, a trace of protein in her urine and some oedema. However, on today's examination things appear to have progressed.'

He pressed a finger lightly into the swollen skin around Amy's ankle, leaving a little dimple in the pale flesh that remained there once he removed the pressure.

'Pitting oedema is now evident, her BP, both systolic and diastolic, has gone up by another 10mmg and the amount of protein in her urine has increased.' He gave Amy a wry smile. 'I'm giving Ms Adams the benefit of the doubt that she didn't have the easiest job getting here today and that could account for the rise in blood pressure. She also assures me that, as of yesterday, she is now officially on maternity leave from her full-time job.' His eyes went carefully from one to the other.

'For the next twenty-four hours I've agreed with Ms

Adams that she requires some careful monitoring. We're going to monitor her blood pressure, her fluid intake and output and do a twenty-four-hour urine collection. So...' he looked directly at Lincoln '...your services aren't required in the immediate future but...' he gave a little nod to Amy '...I'm not ruling it out.'

David took a measured breath, his cool grey eyes resting on Lincoln. 'I'm sure you realise the importance of ensuring Ms Adams has a calm environment. I trust there will be no problems?'

Linc shifted uncomfortably. So David definitely had heard the earlier exchange. And even though his words were phrased as a question, this was a direct instruction.

Linc fixed a smile on his face. 'Absolutely, Dr Fairgreaves. Thanks very much for agreeing to monitor Amy.'

His point made, David's face relaxed and he gave a nonchalant shrug of his shoulders. 'Hey, what else am I doing?' Then he slid out between the curtains.

The silence screamed in Lincoln's ears. She was watching him again, waiting to see what he would say. His hand automatically ran through his dishevelled hair—what he wouldn't give for a shower and a comfortable bed right now. What he really needed was twelve hours' solid sleep, with some serious blackout blinds. But the way his brain was currently spinning, there was no chance of that.

He pulled the chair over again and sagged down into it. 'Okay, Amy. Let's get to it. What's going on here? Where do you normally stay? And what did David mean about maternity leave? Where do you normally work?'

She crossed her hands in her lap. 'Wow, an interrogation. Or is it an interview? Is this how you talk to all your potential patients, Dr Adams? Do I have to pass muster before you'll take my son on as your patient?'

He shook his head. Sleep deprivation was making him ratty. It didn't matter what he'd read in her notes. He wasn't going to make this easy for her. She was going to have to tell him herself. 'This is how I talk to the girl who walked away six years ago without a backward glance, and then turns up when she sees me on television.'

Amy felt her bottom lip tremble. This wasn't going well. She could see he was tired. She knew he would be under extra stress looking after the First Daughter, but perfect timing was the one thing she didn't have here. And she needed the assurance of Lincoln's help now.

'That's not fair and you know it.'

He shook his head in frustration. His voice was quiet but even. 'I know.'

She switched into professional mode. 'Okay, Dr Adams. I normally live in Santa Maria in Butte County—around four hours from here. I work in one of the free clinics there. And my maternity leave started...' she glanced at her watch '...officially around twelve hours ago.'

Her notes were still in his hands. But he wasn't looking at them. It looked as though he hadn't read them. It would be so much easier if he did, then at least he might understand why she'd left.

'Why me, Amy, and why now?'

A loud burr came from the monitor beside her and the electronic blood-pressure cuff started to inflate again. Amy winced as the cuff over-inflated on her arm. Linc watched with alarm as the reading on the monitor climbed higher and higher. One-eighty...one-ninety...two hundred. *Please don't let her blood pressure be that high.*

Amy's voice cut through his thoughts. 'There are a lot of kids currently alive in the Amazon because of you, Linc, and you know it. Kids who would have died if you hadn't been on that boat.'

She saw him bite his bottom lip. Linc was a team player, not a glory hunter. She knew how uncomfortable he'd been in that press interview. He must have said the words 'I have a fantastic team' at least five times. She knew he wouldn't be interested in the chat-show interviews or celebrity magazine spreads that would materialise in the near future.

A black-suited figure crossed the gap in the curtains. She waved her arm. 'Look at all this, Linc. When the First Lady went into premature labour, who did they call? You. They must have been able to get almost any doctor in the world, but they chose you to look after the First Daughter. The first presidential baby in nearly fifty years. What does that tell you?'

'It tells me I was in the wrong place at the wrong time, Amy, nothing else.' He shook his head, 'You make it sound grander that it actually was. Abby Tyler was the admitting physician here in Pelican Cove. She works with me at San Francisco Children's Hospital. They asked her for a neonatologist and she recommended me.'

Amy waved her arms, 'And you're telling me that the whole secret-service brigade out there didn't check your credentials? To make sure that only the absolute best of the best was looking after the President's baby? I seriously doubt that. Hell, the other doctor is an award-winner.'

He smiled at her. 'You'll find it hard to believe, but that was sheer coincidence. David Fairgreaves has a boat moored in Pelican Cove, the man is an old sea dog. Whenever he's here, Abby has an arrangement to call him for any obstetric emergencies. He apparently likes to keep his hand in.'

Amy folded her hands across her chest. 'Oh, come on. You're telling me the secret service didn't check on him too? Especially that old stony-faced one. Does he ever smile?'

Linc laughed at her description of James Turner, the head of the presidential security detail, the original man-in-black. 'I think I've only seen him smile once in the last three days—and that's when he told Luke Storm, one of the other docs, that he couldn't leave. Somehow I think his job must drain all sense of humour from his body. He spends his life looking over his shoulder for potential threats to the Presidential family.'

The blood-pressure cuff stopped abruptly. The hiss of air seeping out from it. Linc glanced at the screen again—150/96. A bit higher than before, but not yet dangerous. Still worth keeping an eye on. His eyes fell to his watch. There were a million things he wanted to say right now. A million things he wanted to know. Six years to catch up on. But David had been right. He had other duties—other priorities—that he couldn't get distracted from.

'I'm sorry, Amy, but I seriously need some shut-eye and I've a neonate to deal with who doesn't want to feed.'

Her eyes fell to the notes, still clutched in his hands. She couldn't hide the slight tremor in her voice. 'Will you read my notes and tell me if you'll agree to be my baby's doctor?' Her hands were back at her stomach, protectively rubbing her extended abdomen.

The notes. She knew exactly what he would read in there. But for some reason he didn't want to give her an easy way out. Why couldn't she just find the words to tell him? She had no idea he'd already read them. And he was beginning to feel too tired to care.

'In the interests of professionalism I'll read your notes, not now—later—but I want to hear everything—straight from the horse's mouth, so to speak. There's nothing in these notes that you won't be able to tell me yourself. I'll come back later. We'll talk then—and I'll decide if I can be your baby's doctor or not. I can't do it if there's going to be a conflict of interest for me, and…' his eyes rolled towards the outside corridor as he gave her a crooked little grin '…your timing could have been better.'

Amy watched as he exited through the curtains, her throat tight.

She needed him. She needed him to be there for her baby—and for her. He was the best in the world. No one else would do. She couldn't lose this baby.

It had all seemed so simple in her head. As soon as she'd known she was at risk of pre-eclampsia, she'd known she had to find Linc. She'd seen him bring neonates that should have died back to life. And that was normal for him.

The long line of mothers who'd queued up on the banks of the Amazon to show them their healthy, growing children—children he had saved in previous years— was testament to that.

There had been no doubt in her mind. This was all about her baby. All about the little boy currently growing in her stomach.

So why was she feeling like a teenager with a schoolgirl crush? She hadn't thought about Lincoln for the last five years.

No. That wasn't strictly true. He'd crept into her dreams on a few occasions—all of them X-rated. But dreams you couldn't control. Truth be told, she hadn't let herself think about playboy Linc for the last five years. Too much potential for heartache. She'd had to concentrate all her energy on beating the cancer.

And now she was only here because she needed him for her son. Really.

When she'd had her detailed scan she almost hadn't asked what sex her baby was. But at the last moment she'd changed her mind. She'd wanted to prepare for her son or daughter. She'd wanted to pick his pram, his bedclothes and the paper for his nursery wall. She'd even picked his name. Zachary. Zachary John Carson.

She whispered the name as her hands ran over her stomach. 'Stay inside just a little longer, Zachary. I need you to be as healthy as can be when you come out. Momma needs to know that you're going to do just fine.' A tear slid down her cheek and the anger started to rise in her chest.

Why should the First Lady's baby be any more important than hers? And why did she, after everything she'd been through, have to develop a condition that could threaten her baby?

But this was it. Cancer had crept through her body tissues and the chemotherapy had ravaged them. She'd lost her ability to have a baby naturally and this embryo was her last chance. Her only chance.

So how come she couldn't just focus on her baby?

From the first second she'd opened her eyes and seen Lincoln again, her heart had gone into overdrive. There were so many things about him she'd forgotten. His intense gaze. His lazy smile. His flirting. The way he could comfort her with the touch of his hand and the stroke of his finger.

And the camouflage he kept around himself.

She'd seen how he jumped from being really comfortable around her one minute, like it had only been a few days since they'd seen each other, since they'd slept together and been wrapped in each other's arms, to shifting into the professional role, the possibility of being her baby's doctor and all the lines that blurred in between.

But she wasn't asking him to be *her* doctor, so surely that simplified things?

So why did her heart keep beating rapidly in her chest every time he was next to her? Why did her hairs stand on end when he touched her and make her feel as if an electrical charge had run up her arm?

Amy squeezed her eyes shut tightly. She couldn't allow herself to feel like this. Lincoln wasn't interested in her. She was a six years past girlfriend who'd had a mastectomy and was carrying a child that wasn't his. Why would he even give her a second glance?

He was only being kind. He was only being a friend. He couldn't possibly want anything else from her, could he?

This was Lincoln Adams. And yesterday this gorgeous blue-eyed, brown-haired doc had been announced on television as looking after the First Daughter. He was world news. Women would be throwing themselves at his feet.

She had to concentrate on the most important thing right now—a safe delivery and outcome for her baby. She'd come here to find Lincoln Adams because he was the best doctor to care for her baby. Nothing else. No matter how he currently made her feel.

CHAPTER THREE

'LINC? Linc?'

The voice was quiet, softly spoken, but the hand pressing down on his shoulder was firm, stirring him from the first hour's sleep he'd had in two days.

'What...what is it?' His hands automatically went to his sleep-filled eyes and he rubbed hard. He looked around him. He'd sat down for just a minute in the NICU, waiting for the First Lady to awaken and try to feed her baby again, but the heat from the unit had enveloped him and before he'd known it...

Val, one of his nurses, was standing next to him smiling. 'Wake up, sleeping beauty, you're needed.'

'Is Jennifer Taylor awake?'

Val nodded. 'She's been awake for the last half-hour. Both Ruth and I have tried to assist her with breastfeeding, but the truth is we just can't get this baby to latch on.' She glanced down at her watch. 'And if we're going to follow the protocols we normally use at San Fran then we're at our time limit for getting some fluids into this baby. You're going to have to come and talk to her.'

Linc gave a nod, stood up and tried to flatten his rumpled scrubs. He walked over to the nearby sink and splashed some cold water on his face and hands.

Neonates could be hard work. Esther, who had been

born at thirty-two weeks, hadn't yet developed her natural mechanism to suck and feed. It was a common complaint in premature babies and one he was used to dealing with. The last thing in the world he wanted to do was to put a tube into the baby's stomach and feed it artificially. The First Lady wanted to breastfeed and he would make sure that he and his staff did everything they could to make that happen.

He pulled some paper towels from the nearby dispenser and dried his face.

'Have you had any success expressing some breast milk?'

Val nodded. 'Ruth's in there with her now—we knew that would be the next step.'

Lincoln took a deep breath and pushed open the door into the adjoining room. Charles Taylor, the President of the United States, was perched on the edge of the bed one arm wrapped around his wife's shoulders, the other cradling daughter Esther. By neonatal standards Esther was a healthy weight at just under five pounds. Would Amy's baby be so lucky? Where had that come from? Lincoln felt a little shudder drift down his spine. He had a job to do. He couldn't allow himself to be distracted.

Jennifer's brow was furrowed, her eyes fixed on the pump that the nurse Ruth was using to help her express some milk from her breasts. She looked exasperated as the smallest trickle of creamy breast milk started to collect in the receptacle.

'What's wrong with me?' she gasped. 'Is that it? No wonder my baby can't feed.'

Lincoln crossed the room in a few steps and sat down at the bottom of the bed. This was no time for pomp and ceremony. The last thing he wanted was for Jennifer to think she was failing at feeding her child.

'Give it a few minutes, Jennifer. Ruth is an expert at this and it takes a bit of time for your milk to come in. Remember, Esther is a tiny baby and she won't need a huge amount to start with.' He pointed at the small amount already collected. 'That is called colostrum. And it's like gold dust for babies. It contains antibodies and is rich in protein and carbohydrates—exactly what your baby needs.'

The tears were already starting to form in Jennifer's eyes. 'But she won't feed. I can't get her to take anything.'

Lincoln nodded. 'And that's entirely normal for a thirty-two-weeker. Her natural instincts to suck and feed haven't kicked in yet. Sometimes it can take a few weeks. In the meantime, we have to look at how to get some fluids into her. The last thing we want is for your baby to dehydrate.'

Jennifer sagged back against the pillows behind her. The effect of the relaxation had an immediate impact on the flow from her breasts. 'Look, there's some more. Once we have a few more mils we'll start to look at an alternative method for getting some breast milk into Esther. Any extra milk we can refrigerate or freeze.'

'But I want to breastfeed. I told everyone I want to breastfeed.'

Lincoln could see the stress on Jennifer's face. He reached out and automatically touched her hand. 'And you will. In the meantime, in order to keep your daughter from screaming the house down, we'll give her your breast milk another way.'

'How?'

'There's two possibilities and it all depends on the baby. We can try cup feeding or finger feeding. What we definitely won't do is put your breast milk into a bottle.'

'I've never heard of these. How on earth can a baby drink from a cup?' She turned to face her husband. 'Have you ever heard of these?'

Charles lifted his eyes from his daughter, still caught in the rosy glow of new parenthood, smitten with his daughter's face. 'Nope, you've got me. Never heard of them.'

Lincoln smiled. 'The word *cup* might not be strictly true. We don't use a regular cup—we use a medicine cup and, to be honest, this type of feeding isn't anything new, it's been around for a long time. We place the edge of the cup at the baby's mouth and bring the liquid up to baby's lower lip, so she can lap it up—a bit like a pussycat. It can get a little messy.' He smiled at Charlie, who still had his suit on. 'We can you give something to change into.' He nodded at Val, who had just detached the breast pump. 'One of us will take some time and teach you how to do it. It can take a little bit of practice to get it right. It does mean, though, that you can both help with Esther's feeding.'

Charlie gave a broad smile. There was no mistaking the joy in his eyes as he looked at his daughter. 'Whatever she needs,' he murmured.

Lincoln watched Jennifer's face. She looked a little easier. 'This is only a temporary measure to help get some fluids into Esther. We'll still try putting Esther to the breast and encouraging her to latch on.'

'Wouldn't it just be easier to put a tube down?'

'In theory it might be. But if we feed Esther by tube and she has the sensation of feeling full, she won't have any motivation to suck. That's what we really need to work on. Feeding by tube would be the last resort and I don't think we'll need to do that.'

Jennifer nodded slowly. 'So how do you know if she's getting enough?'

'We'll monitor her diapers and check the tone and elasticity of her skin.' His eyes caught sight of Val, transferring some of the breast milk into one of the medicine cups.

He stretched his hands out towards Charlie. 'Do you mind if I take her for a minute? We want to be sure and have her wrapped up securely before we start—little hands can make a terrible mess when we're cup feeding.' He smiled at the President's suit. 'Wanna play doctor for the day and change into a set of scrubs?'

Charlie nodded. 'Come with me,' Ruth, the other nurse, said as she headed towards the door. 'I'm sure we can find something for you.'

Lincoln tried hard to focus on the task at hand. Getting the First Daughter to feed should be his first and only priority. So why were his thoughts filled with pale skin and red, curly hair?

The buzz from the monitor and the tightening cuff on her arm woke Amy from her daze. Damn cuff. How was anyone supposed to sleep with this stupid thing going off every thirty minutes? No wonder her blood pressure was rising—she couldn't get any peace and quiet.

A smile crossed her face. Things were different from a patient perspective. She'd never really given much thought before to the electronic monitoring devices that she used as a nurse. Cardiac monitors that beeped incessantly, IV fluid pumps that alarmed when they needed changing and syringe drivers that required hourly monitoring. It was no wonder patients complained.

She turned her head and glanced at the screen beside her. Damn! Her blood pressure hadn't gone down at all. The curtains surrounding her had been pulled tightly and lights around her had been dimmed. What time was it? Was it night-time? It must be—she'd just been about to slip into another X-rated, Lincoln-filled dream. Definitely not suitable for a hospital stay.

She swung her legs from the trolley and reached for her

bag. Somewhere in the depths of this giant tote bag should be her watch—she'd slipped it off earlier when her wrist had felt uncomfortable. She rummaged around inside the bag—lipstick, phone, receipts, purse, umbrella, spare undies, fold-up flat shoes, pens, pens and more pens. Ten minutes later she gave up. She pulled the cuff from her arm, the ripping Velcro echoing around the quiet emergency department. Where had everyone gone?

As her bare feet hit the cold linoleum floor her head swam a little. How long had it been since she'd eaten? Judging from how her stomach felt, it must have been hours. A little gust of cold air struck her back. Blast! She still had on her hospital gown. It fastened down her back and currently felt like fresh-air fortnight back there; thank goodness she had respectable undies on. She grasped the back of her gown in her hands and stuck her head out between the curtains, glancing one way, then the other, out into the eerie silence, before heading towards the nurses' station. It was deserted and according to the white board on the wall she was the only patient currently in the E.R. No wonder it was so quiet around here.

Then the thought struck her. Of course there were no other patients—the President and the First Family were in this hospital. She'd only got in here by default. Fainting at the police cordon could do that for you.

A packet of half-eaten cookies sat on the desk. She looked around again. Still no people. Well, if someone wanted to leave an open packet of cookies unguarded they could take the consequences. She flopped down into one of the nearby chairs and grabbed a cookie, oblivious to the crumbs falling down the front of her hospital gown, and closed her eyes. Bliss.

'Do you always steal the staff food?'

Amy's eyes shot open and she spluttered, which turned into a cough as part of a cookie lodged in her throat.

Lincoln looked amused as he went around behind her and gave her two hard slaps on the back.

She coughed the piece of cookie back up, catching it in her hand before depositing it in the trash can. She held her hands up. 'Guilty.'

She looked around the darkened corridors. 'Where did you spring from? I never even heard you. This place is like a scene from a bad slasher movie.'

Lincoln laughed, looking at the deserted corridors. He pointed to a door down the hallway. 'I came from the staff-room, where the current E.R. staff are watching reruns of the baby announcement. Don't think they've ever had it so quiet. And you...' he pointed at her '...are apparently resting peacefully with a still-borderline blood pressure and signs of pre-eclampsia.'

Amy rolled her eyes. She lifted her leg and stuck it on the nearby chair, prodding around her ankle and then further up her shin. 'I think the oedema is getting worse.'

Lincoln bent his head towards her leg under the dimmed lights. He was so close she could feel his breath on her skin. He ran his hand up and down her leg.

Wow! A physical examination wasn't supposed to feel like that. It wasn't supposed to make your skin prickle and your blood heat. Thank goodness she'd shaved her legs, or the hairs would currently be standing on end!

But what about him? How was he feeling right now? Did he know the effect he was having on her? Lincoln had always had a wicked sense of humour—was he teasing her? Knowing that her insides had currently turned to mush?

'Any oedema around your abdomen?'

His voice broke through her thoughts. So much for illicit daydreams. She bit her lip and shrugged her shoulders. 'To be honest, I didn't really look when I woke up. I was too busy in the hunt for food.'

'Do you want me to get you something to eat?'

'Can you? This place looks as if it's closed down for the night.'

'Aha.' He put a finger to his lips. 'I might only have been here for two days but I prioritised. I made sure I'm best friends with the canteen staff. What do you want?'

Pictures of barbecue chicken breasts, fresh green salads and French fries swam in front of her eyes. Closely followed by images of scrambled eggs and sausages. It was amazing the weird cravings that pregnancy gave you—even in the middle of the night. She sighed. 'To be honest, Linc, I'll take whatever I can get.'

He stretched out his hand towards her in the dim light. She hesitated, just for a second. Was this a doctor-patient thing? No. It wasn't. David Fairgreaves was her doctor. Linc was her friend. Her good friend. A friend she was going to have to persuade to take care of her baby.

She reached up towards his hand. 'You're going to have to heave, Linc, I don't think I can get out this chair.'

He enclosed her hand with both of his and gave her a gentle tug from the low-seated chair. The momentum caught her unawares and she took a few steps forward, her hands coming automatically upwards and resting on his hard chest.

And she stopped.

Both hands were resting on his firm muscle, his face just a few inches from hers. In the dim light she could see his dark-blue-rimmed eyes pulling her in. See his perfect skin, with a light stubble on his chin. Before she knew it, her fingers had moved upwards and touched his shadowed jaw. *This was how her dream started.* A smile broke across his face, his hand moved across her back and she felt two fingers resting lightly at the base of her spine, between the gap in her patient gown. Would he kiss her?

When was the last time she'd felt like this? When was the last time she'd wanted a man to kiss her? To feel his touch on her skin? Her lips tingled, aching to feel his pressing against them. Her tongue ran along them, desperate to give them some moisture and invite him in.

'I don't know if I'm dressed appropriately for the staff canteen,' she whispered.

He looked downwards. His eyes following the gentle swell on one side of her breast. Her breath caught in her throat. Would he look to the other side? Would his face register disgust or displeasure?

Neither. His eyes stayed fixed on one side. As if there was nothing wrong. As if the gap on the other side was the most natural thing in the world. Something lurched inside her and she almost jerked in recognition of what it was. Acceptance. This was her. This was her body shape now. And there was no need to feel ashamed or embarrassed. Her skin flushed. For the first time in a long time she felt like a woman again. His lips brushed against her ear, his voice husky. 'From where I'm standing, you look just fine.'

I'm dreaming. This isn't really happening. I'm still lying on that hospital gurney, waiting for the BP cuff to go off again.

Light spilled across them. The door from the staffroom opened. A person still facing inside and laughing at the jokes stood with their foot jammed in the door, sending bright white light spilling down the corridor towards them.

Lincoln stepped backwards. For a second he looked like the proverbial deer caught in the headlights, before he regained his composure and cleared his throat.

'The canteen,' he said. 'I was going to take you to the

canteen.' It was almost as if he was saying the words out loud to remind himself what he was supposed to be doing.

His hands fell back to his waist and he gave her a nod in the other direction. 'The canteen's this way, Goldilocks. Let's see what we can get you to eat.'

He took a few long strides ahead of her, making short work of the corridor and pushing open the swing door at the other end and holding it open for her.

'I think Goldilocks was a blonde, not a redhead,' she murmured as she followed him, still grasping self-consciously at her gown.

'But look how much trouble she got into for the search for food,' he replied promptly, sending another smile across her face. The easy banter between them was returning as quickly as it had left. Linc was obviously relaxing again. And she was glad. That was when she liked him best.

They stepped into the canteen, which was bathed in the usual bright hospital lights. Amy squirmed, looking around at the deserted tables and chairs. 'Are you sure we can get something to eat?'

Lincoln nodded, smiling at her again as though his moment of discomfort had passed. 'Sure we can. They've got to feed the nightshift, remember?' He ducked behind the counter and into the kitchen beyond. Amy could hear the happy chattering inside and looked at the empty canteen around her. Even this was strange. She was used to sitting in hospital canteens in her uniform, not in a patient gown. On past occasions when she'd had her surgery and treatments she'd never even made it down to the hospital canteens. At that point food had been the last thing on her mind. A few minutes later Lincoln came out, clutching a tray with a teapot and cups.

'Food will be out in a minute,' he said as he set the tray down on the nearest table. Amy gave him a smile. 'I didn't know you were a tea drinker.' She lifted the cups from the tray.

He wrinkled his forehead. 'Generally I'm not. But I didn't want to come out here with a double-shot coffee when you probably aren't drinking it right now.'

His eyes rested on her extended abdomen and she nodded knowingly. 'It's been a slow, hard fight to stop the addiction to the double shots we used to drink.'

His face broke into that easy grin again. The grin he'd given her when it had just been the two of them, standing in the dim E.R. He lifted the lid of the teapot and gave the water a little stir.

The door clanged open behind them and a little grey-haired lady appeared with a plate in either hand. The delicious aroma of food swept around them and Amy's stomach responded by rumbling loudly.

'Oh, wow!' she said as the plate was set before her. 'Thank you so much.' She beamed. The steam was rising from the freshly made pancakes on the plate, with a pile of sausages and scrambled eggs on the side. 'You must have read my mind,' she said accusingly at Lincoln. 'I was dreaming about these earlier.' *Better than telling him what else she'd dreamed about.* She picked up the pepper pot and sprinkled pepper over her scrambled eggs. 'I am so-o-o hungry.'

He sat for a few seconds, watching her. The way her hair fell over her eyes, one delicious auburn curl just begging to be tucked behind her ear. Sitting like this, her extended abdomen was tucked under the table. For a few seconds he could actually forget she was pregnant. Forget she was here, looking for his help because she was afraid she was about to have a premature baby. He could forget the questions spinning in his head about the pregnancy, the conception, the father. All the things he wanted to ask her about. Right now, the clock was spinning backwards in his head. Back to those six precious months when she'd been *his* Amy. Back when they'd been in the first flush of heat and passion. When they hadn't been able to keep their hands off each other. When stifling hot long days had turned into even hotter and longer nights.

The pale green colour of the hospital gown reminded him of the scrubs they'd worn on the boat. A colour that seemed to reflect the darker green of her eyes, drawing his attention to them from the first second he'd seen her.

Damn! He could kick himself. Was there something else he could have done to find her? Why hadn't he insisted on getting her phone number?

The last six years could have been entirely different.

She leaned back in her chair with a contented and relaxed look on her face, her extended abdomen becoming visible again and jolting him back to the here and now. 'Oh, wow, Linc. I don't know who made those pancakes but we should wrap her up, steal her and take her home with us.'

Her eyes flew open and she sat bolt upright. Had she just said that out loud? Oh, no! 'I didn't mean... I mean I wasn't suggesting...' She couldn't find the words, her brain was scrambled at her ridiculous faux pas. Fatigue and irritability had definitely got the better of her. It didn't help that Linc was sitting staring at her with his fork poised frozen just outside his mouth. But he didn't look shocked. He didn't look upset. He looked...amused.

'Relax, Amy,' he said in a teasing tone. 'Don't get wound up. I know what you meant and we certainly don't want your blood pressure getting any higher.' The gleam in his eyes spoke a thousand words that he wasn't saying out loud.

And then he couldn't stay silent any longer. The frus-

tration from earlier in the day came bubbling to the surface and he wanted to hear the words coming from her
lips—not read them in her medical records. 'Why didn't
you come back? You left for a two-week holiday and never
came back. What happened?'

The question jolted her back to reality. No pleasantries.
No niceties. What had happened to playboy, sexy Linc?
This was right at the heart of the matter.

And she'd known at some point he'd ask her. And she'd
practised what she would say in her head. Words that she'd
rehearsed a hundred times in the cab on the way here.
Words that just seemed to stick in her throat.

'Well?' He was still staring at her. With those big dark
blue eyes. She'd seen eyes like that on a model advertis-
ing aftershave once. Everyone had commented on them.
But that guy's eyes weren't a patch on Linc's. That guy
didn't have a dark blue rim encircling his bright blue iris.
Something that pulled you right in and didn't let go. Her
hand ran down his arm and her fingers intertwined with
his. She needed to do this. She needed something familiar.
Something to give her strength right now. It didn't matter
if he had a wife outside. They were friends. Or they *had*
been friends. And right now she needed her friend's support.

She needed to make him understand why she hadn't
come back to the boat. And she already knew how he'd
respond—he'd want to know why she hadn't told him at
the time. But those were all questions she could field. She
needed his skills right now, and his expertise for her baby.

'I was sick, Linc. I couldn't come back.' The words were
faint, almost whispered, and his head jerked upwards from
its focus on their intertwined fingers.

This was where he could make it easy on her and tell
her he'd read her notes. But he didn't want to, he wanted

to hear her say the words. 'What do you mean, you were sick?'

She shook her head, a watery sheen across her eyes. She gave his hand a little squeeze. Why did she have to tell him here? In this hospital canteen in the middle of the night? Why couldn't they be sitting somewhere in private, looking out over that wonderful cove?

She took a deep breath. 'I had breast cancer.' There, she'd said it. The words that no one liked to say out loud. The words that people normally whispered around about her.

His face didn't change. And she almost wished she hadn't told him. But she had to. She had to make him understand why this baby was so important to her. Why this baby was her only chance.

Then he did it. The one thing he used to do all the time. He rubbed his thumb lightly along the palm of her hand. The softest of touches. The most delicate of touches. Like he'd used to do when they'd had a stressful day on the boat. When there had been too many patients and not enough staff. When they hadn't been able to treat everyone they'd wanted to. When patients had got really sick, and some had even died.

His face was serious now. And in amongst all this madness—the press pack outside, the security staff everywhere, him looking after the First Daughter—she knew she had made the right decision. Linc was one of the good guys. He would help her. She could feel it.

He cleared his throat. 'Why didn't you tell me?'

She sighed. 'How could I tell you that, Linc? I went home for a holiday. I had the first proper shower in months and felt a lump under my breast. And I'd no idea how long it had been there. Two days later I had a fine-needle biopsy that told me I had cancer.' Her finger reached up and twiddled one of her long red strands of hair, her other hand still intertwined with his. 'I'd only known you six months. You were on a boat on the Amazon, thousands of miles away. How could I phone and tell you I had cancer and needed treatment?' She flung her arms in the air in an act of exasperation. 'Let's face it, Linc, I was your yearly summer fling.'

He winced at the harshness of her words. So she *had* heard about his reputation. He'd always hoped no one had mentioned that fact that each year he'd had an affair with a colleague on the boat. He wanted to shout out, *Of course you should have told me!* But he understood the futility of the answer. Amy was right. They had only known each other a few months. And life on the Amazon was all-consuming—you lived in each other's pockets and had very little time off. Everything was about the work and the people. Lots of medics had relationships on the Amazon boats, but when they got back to normal life the relationships tended to fall apart as they found they had nothing in common any more. What would he have done if she'd told him? Left the boat? Gone to find her? Would she even have wanted him there?

His anger from earlier felt misplaced. If the shoe had been on the other foot and he was one who had been sick, would he have told Amy?

He wasn't sure and he hated to admit that. Would he really have wanted to put that responsibility onto her? He would have hated it if she'd felt obliged to help him out of an innate sense of duty, especially when he didn't know how she felt about him.

His lips tightened and he gave her hand another squeeze. 'So what happened, Amy?' Although he couldn't help it, his eyes went automatically to her breasts. The professional in him knew better than that. But the personal element kept distracting him. He'd had his hands all over those beautiful breasts. And as for the pink rosy nipples...

He saw her shift uncomfortably, her hands rising to her chest. 'I had a mastectomy on one side.' The words were simple, but they masked how they made her feel. What would Linc think of her body shape now if he could see it? The two of them had danced naked around his little cabin and the memories of that now could make her cry. She could never do that now. Never feel that confident in her body.

'Really?' Now he couldn't avert his eyes because, if she'd had a mastectomy, it wasn't apparent. And he'd only flicked over the treatment plan—he hadn't read it in detail. 'Did you have a reconstruction?'

Her hands self-consciously stayed where they were. And under them she could feel the long-term results of her disease—full, soft breast on one side and a gap on the other side, currently filled with a pale pink silicone breast enhancer. 'I meant to but, no, not yet,' she murmured.

His brow crinkled. 'So what stopped you?' She was a beautiful young woman. It seemed strange she hadn't completed her treatment and moved on to the next part of her life. Most young women he'd ever met, and it was only a few, who'd had breast cancer had had some kind of reconstruction done at a later date.

Amy ran her hands over her baby bulge. 'I haven't really had time to get around to it. But it's in my plans.'

Lincoln's eyes fell again to her stomach. His brain was working overtime, trying to remember dates. If she'd had a cancer diagnosis just after leaving the boat, then undergone surgery and treatment, could she have had five years cancer-free before falling pregnant?

No. It didn't add up. According to his calculations she just fell short. Lots of physicians were wary about the effect pregnancy hormones could have on cancer cells. Was it really wise for her to be pregnant? What age was Amy? Thirty-two? She could have waited another year before doing this. Had someone pushed her into it?

He remembered the empty next-of-kin box in her notes and tried to pull his professional head back into place. 'Do you have a husband? A boyfriend I can call for you?'

She shook her head. 'It's just me, Linc.'

The enormity of the words hit him. She was alone. And while one part of his heart wanted to suddenly break into song, he immediately felt angry. Who had left a woman like this, alone and pregnant, after she'd already been through breast cancer?

He stood up, his voice rising in pitch, 'What do you mean, you're alone? Where's the baby's father? Why isn't he here with you?'

'It's just me,' she repeated, the words almost whispered. Most days she was fine with this. Most days she was confident and sure of herself. Confident in her abilities to be a single parent and to stay on top of her previous diagnosis. But sometimes, just sometimes, particularly when someone made a comment around her, she realised the enormity of the task in front of her. If this baby was born prematurely then she might have to deal with a whole host of complications. How would she feel then? Would she still feel confident in her abilities?

Then there was Linc, standing in front of her and right now looking like her knight in shining armour. But what if he refused to help? What if, over the last six years, he'd met someone, fallen in love and now had a whole host of other responsibilities that meant he wouldn't be comfortable helping her?

She raised her eyes to meet his. 'What about you, Linc? Are you on your own, or are you playing happy families somewhere with a wife and a houseful of kids? Is there a real Mrs Adams?'

She held her breath. Why was this answer so important?

Linc looked momentarily thrown by the question. A flickering parade of a variety of short-term lovers passed in the blink of an eye, ending with an image of an irate brunette. He hesitated then answered, 'No. There's no Mrs Adams. It's just me.'

Amy could almost feel the relief flush over her body. Then curiosity got the better of her. 'So what happened? Did the playboy never meet his match? Haven't you met Miss Right?'

The words hung in the air. She saw a flash of something in his eyes—was it annoyance? Linc looked uncomfortable, as if he didn't know how to answer that question.

'I thought I had. I was engaged a few years ago to girl called Polly, a pharmaceutical rep. We even had the wedding planned. But in the end it just didn't feel right. So I had to end it.' He gave a rueful smile. 'And it wasn't pretty.'

Amy sat back in her chair. 'What happened?' She was fighting the horrible sensation that was creeping across her skin. Lincoln had been engaged. It made her feel sick.

'I called it off just after we'd paid the deposit for the reception, the photographer and the cake. I came home to find my apartment cleared out and samples of wedding cake smeared into my suits.'

Amy's eyes widened. 'Wow. I guess you weren't popular, then. The playboy struck out.'

He paused, stopping his mouth from saying the first words that came into his brain.

Amy Carson had shaken him to the core. He'd been a fool, with a playboy reputation that he hadn't ever meant to earn. It had only been when she'd never come back that he'd realised how special she'd been.

She was joking, he could tell by her tone, but the play-boy jibe had cut deeper than he liked, leaving him feeling distinctly ill at ease. It was too late at night for conversations like these. He looked at the half-eaten plate of food in front of her. 'Do you want anything else?'

She shook her head and rubbed her hands across her stomach. 'I don't think I've got room for any more. Junior takes up more space in here than you think.'

'Junior?' He raised his eyebrow at her. 'That's what you're calling your baby?'

She shrugged her shoulders. 'Well, I know I'm having a boy and I have picked a name, but I want to wait until he's here before I share it. So for the moment he's Junior.'

Lincoln's brow furrowed. 'I'm kind of surprised you found out what you were having. I would have taken you for a surprise kind of girl. We used to call you Miss Unpredictable on the boat.'

'You did?' Her eyes widened. She'd never heard the nickname before and, what's worse, it suited her—or at least it used to. She couldn't afford to be unpredictable any more. Amy's lips tightened. 'I wanted to plan ahead. Decorate the room for the baby coming, pick him some clothes, buy a stroller.' She stared off into the distance. 'I always thought I'd want it to be a surprise too, but when the time came I had to have a few detailed scans and because I work in a hospital where they do maternity care I'm used to looking at scans—it was kind of hard to hide the obvious.'

Lincoln's brow furrowed. 'Why did you need detailed scans? Did they suspect a problem?' He hadn't seen anything in her notes that would have made him think there was something wrong with the baby.

Amy lifted her eyes to meet his and for the first time tonight he noticed how heavy they were. She was exhausted.

She leaned her chin on her hands. 'No. No problem. It's just that the clinic where I had my IVF wanted to keep a close eye on me. My embryos had been frozen for five years and then there was a problem…'

'What problem?'

She sighed. 'I had been planning on using the embryos but I was going to wait until I was five years clear of disease and I'd had my reconstruction surgery.'

'So what happened?'

'The storage facilities were compromised.' She lifted her hands. 'We live on the San Andreas fault. Earthquakes are an occupational hazard.'

'An earthquake? Surely any IVF storage facility made plans for that?'

'Even the best plans can be compromised. The DEWAR tank containing my embryos developed a slow liquid nitrogen leak. Some of my embryos perished in the thawing process but I was lucky. A few good-quality embryos survived and I had to make a decision quickly about what I wanted to do.'

He gestured towards her stomach. 'So you went ahead with implantation before you were ready?'

'I had to, Lincoln. This was my only chance to have a child of my own.' She leaned back in her chair again. Was it the conversation making her uncomfortable or was it something else? That was the third time she'd shifted position in as many minutes. She shrugged her shoulders, 'I'm not really that different from lots of other people who find themselves pregnant before they'd planned to be.'

He shook his head, 'But you are different, Amy. You've got a completely different set of circumstances. You had a disease that threatened your life. This baby didn't materialise out of thin air—or as the result of failed contraception.'

'I know that, Linc.' Her eyes clouded over. 'You can't possibly understand.' Her voice lowered. 'You can't possibly know how it feels to have the world whipped out from under your feet. One minute you think you have your whole life to plan a family, to choose when you have it and with whom. Then the next minute you're asked hard questions and you've got about two minutes to make up your mind—because they have to schedule surgery for you and a whole plan of chemotherapy. And in the meantime the clock is ticking because every second you delay could be the second that means your cancer grows and spreads somewhere it shouldn't. The second that could be the difference between life and death for you.'

Lincoln drew in a deep breath. She was tired, he knew she was tired. It was two o'clock in the morning and she was sitting in a strange place, with symptoms that could affect her baby, and with someone she hadn't seen in six years. So why did it feel as if someone had just fastened a thick fist around his heart and squeezed tightly? Why did the heart-wrenching words she'd just said make him feel as if his stomach had just turned inside out?

She fixed her green eyes on his. 'This was it for me, Linc. This was my only chance to have a baby of my own—and even then there was no guarantee that the embryo would take. But I had to try. I couldn't give up that one chance just because the timing wasn't perfect.'

'And the father?' It was a loaded question, and the one he was most interested in.

She gave a rueful smile. 'I didn't have a significant other when I was diagnosed with breast cancer and I was advised to freeze embryos instead of eggs. So I used a sperm donor. What else could I do?'

A sperm donor. An anonymous man who would never

know he was the father of Amy's baby. Did that make him feel better or worse?

The words were echoing in his head. *She didn't have a significant other when she was diagnosed.* But she could have. She could have had him.

He looked down. The plate of pancakes and scrambled eggs that had seemed so appetising ten minutes ago now seemed to turn his stomach. The last time he'd felt like this he'd been out on the town with his friends and had had no idea how or when he'd got home.

Amy shivered. The hairs on her arms were standing on end. How stupid of him. He was sitting here in theatre scrubs and a white coat and all she had on was a hospital gown. He was an idiot. He pushed his chair back. 'Come on,' he said as he walked around the table and put his arm around her shoulders. 'You're cold. It's time I tucked you into that extremely comfortable hospital gurney and let you get some rest again.'

She rolled her eyes and nodded as she stood up next to him, her small frame fitting perfectly under his arm.

Then something struck him. Amy was wrong. He did know how it felt to have the world whipped out from under your feet.

It had happened to him six years before when she'd gone on holiday and had never come back.

CHAPTER FOUR

LINCOLN glanced at his watch as he strode down the darkened corridor. Twenty-four hours later and he still hadn't left this place. Sleep was apparently for the faint-hearted. At least that's what Val, the nurse practitioner, had told him when she wakened him at 2:00 a.m. to come and help with baby Esther.

Jennifer Taylor was really struggling with breastfeeding. Esther, on the other hand, had taken to cup feeding like a duck to water. She was already sleeping for two-hour stretches, but still showed no interest in latching onto her tear-filled mother.

Lincoln knew that the next few days were crucial in helping establish the feeding and that mother-baby bond. There was also the small issue of the world's press. They had developed a persistent interest in how the premature First Baby was being fed. There was no way he was going to say that even though the First Lady had attempted to breastfeed, it had so far been unsuccessful. What kind of message was that to send? And more importantly how would that make Jennifer feel? If people knew that the First Lady had chosen to breastfeed her baby, it could encourage other expectant mothers to do the same. This was a chance to try and influence other people to give their baby the best start in life.

Then there was the matter of Amy. And how he felt about her being here.

In one way, he was relieved he'd finally seen her again. But circumstances for both him and her weren't great. Had she really just come looking for him again to be her baby's doctor? Or could there be something else?

There was no getting away from the fact she was pregnant, had pre-eclampsia, and in all likelihood would deliver this baby early. But deep down Lincoln really wanted to believe there was more to this. More than just the fact he was a good doctor.

He stopped at the door to the side-room and pushed it gently open. 3:00 a.m. and Amy was sleeping soundly on her side with the arm with the blood-pressure cuff attached lying above the covers. The soft hum of the cuff starting to inflate began and Amy started.

'Damn cuff,' she muttered under her breath.

Lincoln smiled and sat down on the chair next to her bed. She was definitely a restless sleeper. Her brow furrowed and her nose twitched as she lay against the pillows, her long red curls spilling over the covers.

He almost felt guilty watching her like this. But he hadn't had much of a chance to talk to her today and she'd been moved from the E.R. to one of the ward side-rooms for monitoring.

Her eyelids flickered open as the cuff tightened on her arm. 'Linc?' she whispered, peering at him through sleep-filled eyes.

He leaned forward and touched her arm. 'Hi, Amy.'

She didn't move, didn't seem surprised to see him. Instead, she seemed to snuggle even closer into the pillows, as if she was sinking into a dreamlike state. 'Hi, yourself,' she murmured as a smile danced across her lips. 'Did you bring food?'

He blinked and held up his empty hands remorsefully.

'No, sorry.' His eyes flickered around the room to the empty bed table and locker. Amy didn't know anyone here. She wouldn't have had any visitors today. No one to bring her grapes or magazines or the occasional bar of chocolate. Why hadn't he thought ahead? 'Do you want me to go and get you something?'

She grimaced as the cuff reached its tightest point, shifting onto her back. 'No, it's fine really. Just wishful thinking perhaps.'

He smiled and leaned forward. 'Wishful thinking about what?'

She ran her tongue along her bottom lip and shrugged her shoulders. 'That when the hero finally appears he usually brings the sleeping princess some gifts. I was kinda hoping for cookies.'

'So now I'm the hero?'

'You were in my dream…' Her voice trailed off, as if she hadn't really thought about what she was saying. Her eyes fixed on his, which were fixed on the monitor at her side. The thoughts of a medic were written all over his face. So much for dreaming.

'David started me on some anti-hypertensives today.'

He pulled his eyes from the monitor screen—conscious of the fact she'd been watching him. 'And how do you feel?'

He knew better than to rely on readings from instruments when a patient could tell you exactly what you needed to know.

Amy gave a sigh of relief as the cuff released then propped herself up in the bed. She pushed her hair out of her eyes, tucking it behind her ears.

Lincoln fisted his hands, resisting the urge to do it for her.

'Crabbit.'

'What?' That got his attention. *Miss Unpredictable*.

She gave him a wicked smile. 'Crabbit—that's how I feel. I could cheerfully take that blood-pressure monitor and lob it out the nearest window.'

He gave a rueful smile. 'It is kind of noisy.'

'It's not the noise—it's the discomfort. Every time I think I'm about to fall asleep the damn thing goes off again.' She narrowed her eyes. 'I thought hospitals were supposed to be places of rest, Dr Adams?'

'No chance,' he muttered, sagging back in the armchair, his legs and arms flopping in exhaustion.

She raised her eyebrow. 'No rest for the wicked?'

He shook his head. 'I don't know about the wicked but there's definitely no rest for me. I keep snatching a few hours here and there, but I feel as if I'm walking about this place in a trance.'

Amy nodded slowly. It was always like this for a doctor on call. As soon as their head rested on the pillow, their pager would go off again. By the end of their shift they looked like death warmed over.

Although still one of the best-looking men she'd ever laid eyes on, Lincoln looked tired. Bags hung under his eyes, and the little lines surrounding them seemed deeper—more ingrained.

She was angry with herself. Had she forgotten the amount of responsibility he had right now? He must be stressed up to his eyeballs, and her presence here couldn't be helping.

She felt a surge in her chest. Her heartbeat started to quicken. Lincoln was looking tired and vulnerable, but sexy as hell. He was watching her through half-shut lids and it was sending tingling sensations along her skin. Why had she come to find him? Was this only about safeguarding her baby? Or was this about something else?

In the whole six years since she'd left the boat she'd never met anyone else like him. No one else had had the same effect on her that he'd had. And it wasn't just the sexual attraction. It was the friendship, the conversation and the flirting. And she'd missed it. She'd missed it all.

There was no one else about. It was just the two of them. Maybe for five minutes she could forget about things. She could forget that she'd had breast cancer. She could forget about the problems with her pregnancy. She could just be Amy. And he could just be Linc.

She pulled the cuff from her arm.

Lincoln watched as she lifted the covers and slid her legs to the side of the bed, turning to face him. Long, slim, white legs with only the tiniest bit of oedema around her ankles. And red-painted toenails with tiny silver stars.

He'd forgotten about that. He'd forgotten that she loved nail art and although, as a nurse, she couldn't have it on her fingernails, he'd never seen her toenails without it.

'Nice stars,' he murmured, his eyes fixated on her toes. She slid forward to the edge of the bed, the loose T-shirt she was wearing hitching up around her hips and sliding down one of her shoulders. The movement gave him the tiniest glimpse of bright pink panties. The lights in the room were dimmed—to let her sleep whilst still being observed by the nursing staff. Her tangled red hair was loose around her shoulders, creating a perfect frame for her white skin and dark green eyes. Something had changed. Something was different.

His breath hitched in his throat. It was how she was looking at him. Her gaze was intent and he heard her take a deep breath and let the air out slowly through her pink lips. For the first time since he'd met her two days ago she didn't seem afraid. She didn't seem worried. She seemed strong and self-confident.

Her hand reached over and took his. 'So, Lincoln...' Her voice was low, husky. 'If you're so tired, what are you doing here in the middle of the night, visiting me?'

He heard the words, but was too captivated by the picture in front of him to answer. A smile appeared on her lips and she turned his hand over in hers, running her fingertips lightly across his knuckles then across his palm. Did she know what she was doing?

She moved his hand towards her body and rested it firmly on her hip. Yes, she knew exactly what she was doing. Amy lifted her hands to his head, running her fingers through his tousled hair. He let out a groan, his other hand automatically lifting to cradle her other hip. He closed his eyes as her fingers trailed over the top of his head and down towards his neck.

The sensations igniting within him were spurred by memories of the past. Six years he'd waited for this. Six years he'd waited to have her in his arms again. He ignored the tiny red flags in his brain. The ones that tried to make him think rationally. Right now he didn't care about professional boundaries. Amy wasn't his patient—and never would be. Her touch was like a drug. His sleep-deprived brain was addicted. His head and neck were on fire underneath her fingertips and he wanted more, he wanted to be closer.

It was instinct. Pure instinct. He heard her feet touch the floor in front of him and he pulled her towards him, lifting his head as she bent hers to meet his.

There was nothing unsure or unconfident about this kiss. Her lips met his, full and plump, kissing him as if her life depended on it. His lips parted as her tongue entered his mouth and he pulled her closer. He ignored the extended abdomen and pushed his hands up the length of her back and into her tangled hair.

Ringlets. Little spirals. That's what he felt. On a lazy day he would have lain next to her in the bed, pushing his fingers gently into her hair, teasing the curls. Tonight he just wanted to touch her hair. Mess it up. Feel it between his fingers again. Remember everything about what it felt like to touch.

And her skin. He wanted to feel her soft, smooth skin. His hand fell to her bare shoulder, running along the curve of her neck, across her delicate bones and back again to the base of her neck, where his fingers danced lightly across her skin again. She gasped, her legs wobbling, her lips releasing from his and her eyes catching his in the dim light. 'Oh, Linc,' she groaned, 'you *know* what that does to me.'

And he was there. Caught in this moment. Mesmerised by the woman before him. His hands curved around her back, sliding under her T-shirt, his fingertips dancing up and down her spine like butterfly wings. His lips touched her ear, his voice deep with desire. 'I remember *exactly* what this does for you.'

Amy tipped her head back, revealing the pale skin on her neck as he bent his head towards her. This was just like the dream she'd had. This was exactly what Lincoln had been doing to her. Only this time it wasn't in her imagination. It was real. She could feel him. She could smell him. She could *taste* him.

And nothing tasted as good as this.

Well, maybe almost nothing.

Her hands dipped lower. He was still wearing the hospital-issue scrubs. The lightest, flimsiest material in the world. She could feel him pressing against her. But it wasn't enough. She wanted to touch him.

Her hands slid beneath the thin material, to what she

imagined was his trademark white jersey boxers under-neath. A surge of pleasure swept through her as she felt his back stiffen and his breath catch as she touched him. Running her fingers up and down his length. When had the last time been she'd felt this much in control? When had the last time been she'd had any sort of sexual encoun-ter? Had even thought of sex?

This was exactly how she remembered it. Every plea-surable second.

His hands swept around from her back towards her breasts. Towards her *breast*. And she stopped. Her heart beat furiously against her chest. Panic overtook her.

She'd been so busy thinking about other things, she'd forgotten about this. She'd forgotten about the fact she was no longer a whole woman. Her hands jerked back from where she'd been holding him. Back to her breasts. Back to her *breast*.

Lincoln froze, feeling her instant stiffening and her pull away from him. What was wrong? He didn't want this to stop. He didn't want this to stop at all.

'Amy?'

He lifted his head from her neck and pulled back, watching her in the dim light. She looked stricken and her cheeks were tinged with pink. She was embarrassed? Why on earth would she be…?

Then it hit him like a blow to the head as he realised how her hands were positioned. He lifted his finger to her pale cheek and stroked it gently as a slow, silent tear slipped down it.

He moved forward, this time to sit alongside her at the edge of the bed and put his arm around her shoulders. She was trembling.

'I'm sorry,' he whispered, 'I didn't think. I just acted on instinct.' He pulled her closer and dropped a kiss on her head as she rested it against his shoulder. 'But you should know, Amy, that it doesn't matter to me.'

He could hear her breathing, ragged and uneven. So he held her closer, wrapping both arms around her. His mind was whirling. Was this his fault? Had he taken advantage of her?

No. He didn't think so. She'd seemed sure. Confident about what she was doing.

Her hand reached over and squeezed his. 'I wasn't thinking either. I haven't been close to anyone since I had my surgery. I didn't know what to expect.'

Linc stepped in front of her, cupping her face with his hands. 'I wasn't trying to make you uncomfortable. I would never do that to you.'

She nodded. 'I know that, Linc, it's just that…I'm not comfortable with it yet. I don't feel right. I don't feel normal.' The tears were flowing freely down her cheeks now. She looked down her uneven frame. 'This just doesn't feel like me.'

Her voice was shaking as she struggled to get the words out. 'And now with everything else…'

He brushed one of the tears from her cheek. 'I know this is hard. But you're still Amy. You're still little Miss Unpredictable that I met six years ago on the Amazon.' He pointed a finger to the centre of her chest. 'I don't need to tell you this, but it's what's in here that counts—not what's outside. Look how many kids we worked with on the boat who had facial abnormalities, what did we tell them?'

She collapsed back against the bed, her head in her hands as the sobs racked her body. 'But that's just it, Linc, I feel like such a fraud. I said all those words to those kids. But now that it's me, I don't believe them, I don't believe them in here.' She prodded at her heart. 'I don't want to be like this. I want to have my body back. The one I'm comfortable in. I had my surgery planned—I even had a date set. Then this…' she pointed at her stomach '…other stuff happened and everything else had to go on hold.'

'Have you ever spoken to someone about this?' Linc's professional head was pulling into focus. This sounded like someone who hadn't really come to terms with what had happened yet.

And he was used to this. Used to dealing with patients and their families. Used to seeing women who had healthy pregnancies then, for unknown reasons, went into premature labour and often had to deal with very sick babies with a whole range of complications. The counsellor attached to his NICU in San Francisco was one of the most essential members of staff. His unit couldn't function without her.

He walked over to the bathroom and grabbed some toilet tissue, handing it to Amy and sitting back down on the bed beside her. 'I'm sure there is someone who you will be able to talk to about this.'

Amy pushed herself up on the bed and blew her nose. 'I've tried, Linc. I went to a local group. It was all women who had breast cancer. But I just didn't fit in. There were some really strong personalities—some women were really against any type of reconstructive surgery. They thought you should embrace the fact you'd had a mastectomy and beaten the disease.' She shook her head. 'But that just wasn't me. It wasn't how I felt about things.'

Linc touched her arm. 'But there has to be more than one group. Maybe you could try another one, with different personalities?'

Her hands settled over her stomach and she raised her red-rimmed eyes to meet his. 'It's more than that. When you touched me…' Her voice faded out.

'What? When I touched you, what?' He didn't want to push, but right now it was clear that Amy needed to talk.

She buried her head in her hands again. 'It didn't feel right. When you used to touch me, I loved the feel of your hands on my breasts. This time your hands came round and I expected what I used to feel. Except this time I felt nothing. It was like a big blank. I wasn't ready for that.'

Lincoln bit his lip. 'Amy, the part of you that's missing is important. You had a huge amount of nerve endings and fibres that just aren't there any more. So it will feel different when someone touches you.'

She lifted her hand and pressed it against her absent breast. 'But I didn't know it would feel like *this*.'

Linc lifted his hand. A loose curl was dangling in front of her face and he brushed it aside, tucking it behind her ear. He gave her a little smile. 'Maybe it's time to relearn things. Maybe you just have to take it slow.'

Amy's hands fell to her extended abdomen. 'I just feel as if there's so much going on right now.' Her hands stroked up and down her bump. 'I don't know if I can do all this at once. I'm so worried about the baby. My blood pressure isn't getting any better and I'm worried about an early delivery. David said he would review me again in the morning, but I can already tell that the symptoms aren't getting any better.'

Lincoln tucked his arm back around her shoulders. 'Don't focus on the bad, focus on the good. Your symptoms haven't got any worse, that's what's most important here.'

She nodded and leaned her head against his shoulder again. 'I know that, but I still can't help worrying.' She reached over and placed her palm on his chest. 'And it doesn't help that the best neonatologist in the world still hasn't told me if he'll look after my baby.'

Lincoln threaded his fingers through hers. 'Amy, of course I'll look after your baby. That was never in any doubt.'

'Promise?'

'Promise.' He stood up, straightening his scrubs and bent forward, lifting the covers and sweeping her legs back up onto the bed. He glanced at his watch. 'Now, Ms Carson, you should be getting some rest.' He picked up the discarded blood-pressure cuff and fastened it back onto her arm. He raised one eyebrow at her. 'Keep it on—doctor's orders. And I'll come back and see you in the morning while David is here.'

Then, just when it seemed he'd reverted back to doctor mode, he stopped and looked at her. She could see the dark blue rims around his eyes. He was watching her. And it seemed as if there were a million things going on his brain, a million things still unsaid. 'Just tell me what you want from me.'

She opened her mouth. She couldn't say what she wanted to. She couldn't say that she wished she could turn back the clock six years and pick up the phone to call him. She said the easiest thing that came to mind. 'I need you to be my friend right now, Linc.' The air deflated from her lungs. This was so *not* what she wanted to say. But anything else right now just seemed too hard.

His lips turned upwards, but the smile was almost... disappointed. The heat and passion that had been in his eyes earlier had vanished. Now his eyes seemed cool, resigned to their fate. He lifted his hand and his finger stroked the side of her cheek. 'Night-night, Amy.'

She turned on her side and snuggled under the covers. 'Night-night, Linc.'

He headed towards the door, pulling it gently shut behind him before taking a few strides down the corridor.

He stopped for a second and leaned against the concrete wall. The coolness spread through his thin scrubs to his heated skin. What was he doing? No—what had he just *done*? His brain was spinning. Should he have professional boundaries with Amy if he was going to take care of her baby?

Did that mean he should step away from her completely? Let some other doctor take care her and her imminent arrival?

He banged his head on the wall. Maybe that would knock some sense into him. Ever since he'd set eyes on her again, she had been all he could think about. Every time he was in the same room as her he just wanted to touch her.

Now he'd just agreed to look after her baby.

But how could he have said no? How could anyone in his position have said no?

Right now Amy needed him. But not in the way he wanted. She wanted to be friends. Friends? Could he do that?

The blood was still coursing through his veins from her earlier touches. The cool concrete wall was doing nothing to soothe the heat emanating from his skin.

He glanced at his watch again. The one thing that Lincoln really needed right now was a good night's sleep. A chance to clear his head and sort out his thoughts. He glanced back towards the dim light filtering out from under her door. But what were the chances of that?

Amy huddled under the covers as the damn cuff started to inflate again. Her body couldn't stop trembling.

She'd kissed him. She'd kissed Linc again. And it had been every bit as wonderful as she'd imagined it to be.

She'd touched him. She'd felt the strong muscular planes of his body under her fingertips.

The tears started to fall again on her already damp pillow. And he'd touched her. And said it didn't matter to him. He hadn't run screaming from the room because she'd had a mastectomy. He hadn't cared that she wasn't a whole woman any more. He didn't even seem to care that she was carrying an anonymous donor's baby.

But did he mean any of it? Because he might have touched her—brushed against her almost—but he hadn't *seen* her.

Lincoln had always been a gentleman. He'd always been a man with a good heart. Was he taking pity on her because of her current predicament?

Or could he really look at her as a real woman?

Amy pulled the covers up around her head. Maybe if she didn't think about this stuff right now it would go away. Maybe this was all just a bad dream and she would wake up in the morning, six years in the past, in her own apartment, ready to return from her holiday to the Amazon aid boat and her hot new doctor friend.

If only…

Lincoln had told her to focus on the good things. Not to think about the bad. She started to count them off in her head. So far, all her cancer check-ups had been clear. In a few months' time she'd reach the golden 'five years cancer-free'. She was being looked after by one of the best obstetricians in the country. There. Two already. This wasn't so difficult.

The finest neonatologist she knew had agreed to look after her baby. She'd just had the most erotic kiss she'd experienced in six years. She'd just felt like a woman again for the first time in six years.

Her mind drifted. Dark tousled hair. Electric blue eyes with a dark blue rim. Broad shoulders and firm, hard pecs.

Amy groaned and pulled the pillow over her head.

Linc. All about Linc. This clearly wasn't working.

'Dr Adams, a word, please.'

Lincoln glanced over his shoulder and heaved a huge sigh. James Turner was standing behind him with his arms folded tightly across his chest. He was quite possibly the last person Linc wanted to see right now. His temper was short and his nerves frayed. Not to mention there wasn't a single thought in his head that currently made sense.

'What word do you want, Mr Turner? How about "busy", "hungry" or "tired"? I'll let you pick.' He closed the notes he was writing in and stood up, sliding them back into the filing cabinet.

James's face remained fixed. 'She has to go.'

Lincoln turned to face him. 'Who has to go?' It was late, his brain was buzzing and he had about ten other things to do right now.

'Your friend Amy Carson. She fainted and now she's better. It's time for her to go home.'

'Really?' Lincoln raised his eyebrow as he tried to control his temper at the sheer cheek of the man. 'And what makes you think that's your decision?'

'I'm in charge of the security for the First Lady. Everything around here is my decision. And I don't make compromises.'

Lincoln stepped forward until he was only inches from James's face. 'I don't like what you're inferring.'

'I don't care.'

'Well, in that case show me your medical degree, *Mr* Turner. Because unless you've got one, I think you'll find this is a medical decision—not a security decision.'

James scowled at him and shook his head. 'Don't make this into something it's not, Dr Adams. This isn't a medical decision, this is personal. Your lady friend turned up here to see you and blagged her way in. She shouldn't be here and she's compromising the safety of the First Lady and the First Daughter, so she has to go.'

Lincoln felt a red mist start to descend over his eyes. He jerked open the door of the filing cabinet and pulled Amy's notes back out. He didn't need to flick through them—by this point he knew them off by heart. 'Let's see. Ms Carson has protein in her urine, her blood pressure is above normal and pitting oedema is evident in her legs and abdomen. She is showing classic signs of pre-eclampsia.' He slammed the notes shut. 'She is at risk. Her baby is at risk. She didn't blag her way in here, Mr Turner, she's been admitted to this hospital because she's sick.'

'She can't be sick here, it's a security risk.'

'Don't be so ridiculous. Is there a pecking order here? Did I imagine it or did the doctors here tell me that you pulled up outside with the First Lady in labour, with no warning, no prior planning? Did you get turned away? Is the First Lady's baby more important than Ms Carson's? Is that the way things have become in the US?'

James pulled a stick of gum from his pocket and popped it in his mouth. 'So transfer her.'

'What?'

'Transfer her somewhere else. They can look after her.'

The man was inhumane. Linc wondered if he was actually a machine. James was immune to anger—he obviously enraged everyone he came into contact with. It was time for a new angle. Lincoln took a deep breath and leaned against the filing cabinet. 'Fine. But if she goes, I go. I've agreed to be her neonatologist. I need to be there when she delivers. And to be frank, I don't care where that is. Make the arrangements, Mr Turner, let me know when we leave.' He turned away and started walking down the corridor. He got six strides before he heard the voice behind him.

'You can't be serious.'

Linc turned back towards the incredulous voice. James had followed him along the corridor. 'You're going to walk away from the First Lady? It's the best publicity you'll ever get,' he sneered.

Linc smiled. 'And if you've done your homework, Mr Turner, you'll know that I'm the doctor that doesn't like publicity and doesn't want it.' He tilted his chin. 'So what's it to be, Mr Turner? Because I'm too tired to fight with you about it. Do you want to arrange the transfer or not?'

James hesitated for a second. Lincoln could see a tiny muscle twitching under his eye. He was furious and Lincoln couldn't have cared less.

He let out a sigh. 'Okay, she can stay.'

'Finally, something we agree on.' And before he could answer Lincoln walked into the on-call room and slammed the door.

CHAPTER FIVE

DAVID stood at the bottom of the bed, his forehead puckered with a frown. 'Can you recheck her blood pressure manually, please?' He nodded to one of the nearby nurses.

He scribbled something in the notes before giving Amy a little smile. 'I'm a bit of a traditionalist.' He gestured towards the monitor. 'Some studies have shown that automated methods can underestimate systolic blood pressure, so I like it double-checked with a mercury sphygmomanometer. Trouble is, in the world of technology they can be hard to find these days.

He glanced back at Amy. 'Yesterday's blood results were fine, but I want to see what today's are like.' He lifted the bed covers and examined her legs and ankles, before unhooking the stethoscope from around his neck. 'Can I take a listen to your chest, please?'

Amy nodded and leaned forward as he lifted her T-shirt, placing his cool stethoscope on her skin. 'Take a deep breath, please.'

Amy breathed in and out slowly as the stethoscope moved from under her breast to her back.

The nurse appeared back at the door with a manual sphygmomanometer in her hand. She took a few seconds to wind it around Amy's arm before inflating the cuff then placing the stethoscope inside her elbow. A few seconds passed before she released the valve and turned to David. 'Same as the machine. One hundred and fifty over one hundred.'

David gave a sigh and stood back.

Lincoln appeared at the door. 'Knock, knock.' He walked into the room, 'How are things, David?

'Your friend Ms Carson is proving quite an enigma.' He pointed at her chart. 'Her blood pressure is still borderline despite her being started on anti-hypertensives yesterday. There's still some protein in her urine. But her lungs are clear and her peripheral oedema seems to be improving.'

He turned back to Amy. 'Any other symptoms?'

She shook her head.

'Then we have a problem.'

'What?' Lincoln's head shot upwards. 'What do you mean, there's a problem?' He moved over to the side of the bed next to Amy.

David gave a little smile. 'In normal circumstances, at this stage, I would probably ask Amy to rest at home and come into the hospital every day to be monitored.'

Lincoln's brow wrinkled. 'I don't understand. What's the problem?'

David gave his shoulders a little shrug. 'It's my understanding that Amy doesn't stay around here. I can't exactly send her home and ask her to come in every day for monitoring if she lives four hours away.'

Amy nodded her head in relief. Thank goodness. For a second there her heart had been in her mouth—she'd wondered what David was about to say.

'But isn't it best she stays here if she's at risk of pre-eclampsia?' Lincoln looked agitated.

David shook his head. 'Not at this stage. Her symptoms aren't severe. Her blood pressure is still borderline and we've started her on some treatment.' He gave Amy a serious look. 'However, you still require careful assessment, daily blood and urine tests, and blood pressure monitoring. We also need to keep a close eye on you to ensure you don't develop any other symptoms.'

Amy gave him a smile. 'So what do you suggest, Dr Fairgreaves?'

'I suggest I give you a little more freedom.'

Amy's smile broadened. 'That sounds good.'

David gave a final glance at his chart. 'For the moment I'm going to recommend your blood pressure is monitored four-hourly. I'm still recommending rest for you. But I don't think a gentle walk outside in the fresh air will cause you any problems.' He gave Lincoln a little nod. 'Providing, of course, you have some supervision.'

Lincoln nodded his head in agreement. 'I think I can manage that.'

'I thought you might.' David touched Amy's shoulder. 'I'll come back and review things later once your blood test results are available. In the meantime, enjoy the sunshine.'

David turned and walked out the door, leaving Lincoln and Amy staring at each other.

'I don't know if I'm happy about this.'

'What's wrong, Linc, scared to take a girl to lunch?'

Linc folded his arms across his chest. 'You make that sound like a challenge.'

'It was. I know you won't be able to resist. You were always a sucker for a challenge.'

His eyes went over to the nearest window. In the last seventy-two hours all he'd seen of Pelican Cove had been the inside of this hospital. White walls and pale grey floors. The thought of getting out into the sunshine and down onto the nearby beach definitely appealed. Fresh air and the smell of the ocean, just like back home at Fisherman's

Wharf. He couldn't think of anything better. Amy looked as if she could do with a change of scenery too. Being hospitalised was enough to send anyone crazy. He gave her a wink. 'I have a baby to check on. I'll be back for you in an hour.'

Lincoln picked up baby Esther from the crib in NICU. She opened her pale blue eyes and scowled at him, her tongue automatically coming out and lapping. He sat down in the nearby chair and picked up her chart. 'Hungry again, little lady? How about trying to latch onto your mom?'

Val appeared at his side. 'She's still being a little madam. We're trying to get her to latch on every time she's due a feed. But she's still not managing.'

Lincoln ran his fingers over the thick dark hair on her head, checking her fontanel, laughing as her tongue came out again. 'Let's take you to Momma and see how you do.'

He went into the room next door where Jennifer was lying on her bed, staring out the window. She sat up as soon as Lincoln came in carrying her daughter.

'Hi, Dr Adams. Is my girl looking for food again?' Jennifer swung her legs out of the bed and moved over into the nursing chair, settling a pillow on her lap and holding her arms out to take Esther. She arranged Esther comfortably and lowered her nursing bra to reveal her dark nipple, and spent the next few minutes trying to get Esther to latch on. Lincoln moved over to her side. 'Would you like to try another position?'

Jennifer rolled her eyes. 'What do you suggest? I've tried the cradle hold, the cross cradle hold, the football hold and the side-lying position. If you've got any others, feel free to tell me.'

Lincoln put his hand on her shoulder in reassurance. 'I know this is hard, Jennifer, but just persevere. Every time she's due to feed, put her to the breast and eventually her sucking reflex will kick in. Look at the way she's extending her tongue. She's doing really well with the cup feeding and she's almost regained her birth weight. She's only lost a few ounces—that's really good for a premature baby.'

He watched as Esther wrinkled her nose and started to wail in frustration, one little arm escaping from her blanket and pushing upwards. 'Here,' he said, taking her from Jennifer and wrapping her firmly in the pale pink blanket again. 'Let's try again for a few more minutes and if it doesn't work, I'll go and get you some of the milk you expressed earlier.'

Jennifer nodded and sat patiently while Lincoln tried to help her latch baby Esther onto her breast. After a few false starts Esther eventually tipped her head backwards and enclosed her mouth around her mother's nipple, but only for a few seconds.

Jennifer gave an exasperated sigh. 'No one tells you it's going to be this hard.'

Lincoln nodded. 'It is hard.' His eyes had a knowing glint in them. 'And although I've had no personal experience, from what I hear, when it does work nothing can compare.' He fixed her with one of his dazzling grins.

Jennifer shook her head. 'You're an incorrigible flirt, you do know that, don't you?'

Lincoln rolled his eyes. 'Me?' He pointed at his chest in mock horror. 'Never.'

She sighed. 'You are. There should be a licence against men like you. You're all big blue eyes and movie-star smiles. The nurses around here are practically falling on their feet around you. How many nurses' numbers have you got in your phone?'

Lincoln had the good grace to look embarrassed. 'None.

Well—none from Pelican Cove,' he added. 'Anyway, Val and Ruth don't give me a second glance.'

She laughed. 'That's because they know you. They've obviously developed an immunity to you. It's all those other poor souls that haven't met you before I feel sorry for.'

She looked at him carefully. 'You don't even know you're doing it, do you?'

Lincoln gave a shrug and picked up one of her apples from the nearby fruit bowl, taking a big bite through the green skin. 'I don't know what you're talking about.'

He gave her a few seconds to think, as he looked around the room. Presents for the baby had been arriving from all around the world.

'Looks like you're going to need a room just for the presents soon.'

Jennifer looked embarrassed. 'Yes, I know. They've come from everywhere. There's no way in the world I'll be able to use all of this. If I'd been in Washington, one of my aides would have taken a note of them all, so we can send thank-you notes.' She bit her bottom lip. 'But I had a bit of temper tantrum and insisted all the aides leave. And I haven't had time to even look at most of them. I'm sure I can find a good home for some of these things.' She picked up the nearest parcel, with beautifully knitted matinee jackets in white and pink. 'What about the NICU? You work in there, Lincoln, could they use some of these?'

He gave her a smile. 'I'm sure we could. San Francisco has lots of families that need some support. Our unit often has to do fundraising so all donations are gratefully received.'

Jennifer eyes swept over the room. 'I've no idea what kind of thing would be best for your unit. Do you want to give me a list?' She pointed towards the door, where the latest pile of parcels had just been delivered. 'And I'm ter-rified in amongst all this stuff there's going to be a present from my Great-Auntie Bertie that I'll miss, or something from my third cousin twice removed.'

Lincoln laid a gentle hand on her arm. 'Maybe it's time to relent and tell James Turner you want one of your aides back. These presents look like a full-time job.'

Jennifer frowned. 'They do, don't they.' She bent her head as she adjusted her daughter in her arms. 'And to be honest, I want to spend my time concentrating on Esther.'

'That's the way it should be.'

Jennifer looked up again. 'If there's anything you want to take in the meantime—I mean, if there's anything you think the people in Pelican Cove might need—just take it.' She waved her arm, 'It's not like I'll miss it.'

Lincoln gave a wry grin. 'Actually, there is something, but it's not what you think.'

Jennifer raised her eyebrow in interest. 'Really? Now, that sounds fascinating. What is it?'

Lincoln bent over and picked up a battered sunhat from beside the bed. 'Can I borrow this? I'm taking a friend for lunch and I think she might be a little unprepared. A sun-hat would be perfect.'

A knowing smile spread over Jennifer's face. 'Would that sunhat be for a pregnant pale-skinned redhead?'

Lincoln started. 'How on earth…?'

She tapped the side of her nose. 'I'm the First Lady, Linc. I know everything.' She laughed. 'Actually, does she need some maternity clothes? I've got a whole wardrobe full that I won't need. Help yourself.' She pointed to the wardrobe in the corner of the room.

Lincoln wrinkled his nose. He hadn't even thought about clothes. And truth be told, Amy probably needed more than a sunhat. Would she be offended if he took her some of the First Lady's maternity clothes? No. He didn't think so.

He gave a little nod. 'Actually, that might just be perfect. Now, let's see if we can get Esther latched on again.'

Amy was sitting on the edge of her bed, wearing the same white smock top and maternity jeans she'd had on three days ago when she'd been admitted. Her eyes widened in shock as Lincoln burst through the door, having changed into jeans and a T-shirt, his arms jammed with clothes, which he dumped on the bed next to her.

'What on earth...?'

'Sorry I'm a bit late,' he said breathlessly. 'I was checking on the First Baby and Jennifer asked if you'd like some of her maternity clothes. She says she won't be needing them any time soon. I hope you don't mind—I said yes on your behalf. I wasn't sure if you'd brought any more clothes with you.' Lincoln held his breath. Had he just committed a huge female faux pas?

Amy turned and looked at the pile of clothes next to her, fingering the expensive fabrics of the designer clothes. 'Wow!' she whispered, as she took in the wide range of styles and colours. Her dark green eyes turned to Lincoln, who breathed a huge sigh of relief. She wasn't angry. Instead, she looked like a child in a sweetie shop. 'She said I could have all these?'

Lincoln nodded and shrugged his shoulders. 'She wanted someone else to have the use of them. She thought you were probably the same size as she is.'

Amy nodded and picked up a summer dress embroidered with tiny flowers. She held it up next to her. 'What do you think Linc?'

'Will it go with this?' He held up the battered summer hat. 'This is what I originally asked for—thought you might need it out there.' He pointed out the window at the blistering sunshine. 'Looks like we're in for a scorcher.'

Amy was rummaging through the clothes on the bed and pulled out a pale green bolero cardigan to match the summer dress. 'Perfect!' she exclaimed, before heading off to the bathroom. 'Just give me a few minutes until I get changed.'

'Take all the time you need,' murmured Lincoln at her retreating back. This was the Amy he knew. Happy and bubbling with excitement. When had the last time been he'd seen her like that?

A vision from the night before flashed in front of his eyes. Images of a beautiful redhead with seduction in her eyes. And he quickly shook it off. This was Amy Carson— friend. Not Amy Carson—former lover. He had to keep things amicable between them. More importantly, he had to keep his mind from wandering.

Amy pushed open the bathroom door, a broad smile across her face. 'Well, Linc, what do you think? Do I look like First Lady material to you?' She swished her flouncy dress, which came to just above her knees, from side to side.

Lincoln tried to stop his mouth from falling open. Pretty as a picture. The words danced around his mind. The dress fitted perfectly, with the cardigan over her shoulders to stop her fair skin from burning and her curly red hair framing her face. His eyes fell automatically to her legs. There was only the slightest amount of oedema around her ankles. A non-medic wouldn't even notice and that was a good sign. He tossed her the sunhat. 'Here you go, don't want you getting scorched out there in the sun.'

She laughed and stuck the hat on her head. 'Have you got any food?'

'Have I got any food?' Linc let out a hearty laugh, 'Amy,

when have you *ever* known me to go anywhere without food?' He pointed to the door, where a small picnic basket sat on the floor, with a picnic blanket tucked under the handle.

'Where on earth did you get that from?'

'The kitchen staff. They love me. No, no, you don't.' He whipped the basket back up as she attempted to open the cover and peer inside. 'You don't get to look until we are sitting comfortably on the beach. *Then* you get to look.'

'If you're going to make me wait it had better be good, mister.' She folded her arms across her chest. 'How far away is the beach anyway?'

Lincoln picked up another bag he'd left at the doorway. 'Apparently about two minutes down a path at the side of the hospital. Or we can take the path at the other side and head down to the harbour. Neither is too far and you should be fine, so take your pick.'

'The beach. Definitely the beach. I can't remember the last time I smelled the ocean.' She wrinkled her nose. 'I don't think I could take the smell from the fishing boats today.'

Linc gave her a smile and extended his arm towards her. 'Then let's go.'

Nope. She wasn't imagining it. There were definitely tingles shooting up and down her arm. Her hand was tightly enclosed in his as he led her down the stone path towards the beach. It wasn't particularly steep, or treacherous, but there was something nice about holding hands. Something familiar and yet intimate at the same time.

The beach already had a number of families set up for the day, with chairs and blankets spread out across the sand, and numerous little kids running around covered in white sunscreen, carting buckets filled with sea water across the sand. Linc pulled the blanket from the under the handle of the hamper and spread it on the sand. 'Is here okay with you?' he asked.

Amy nodded and settled down on the blanket. She slipped off her sandals and buried her toes in the sand. Bliss.

She shaded her eyes from the glare of the sun, already beating down on her pale legs. Thank God she'd thought to pack some factor fifty. It was a gorgeous day, but she didn't want to end up frying in the sun. Her fingers caught the fine cotton material of her dress—the First Lady's dress—and a little smile appeared on her face. The pale green material, dotted with tiny pink, blue and cream flowers, was gorgeous, the style perfect for her extended abdomen. She couldn't have picked a more perfect dress if she'd tried.

With the hat firmly on her head and the cardigan protecting her shoulders, she leaned back on her hands and looked out over the ocean waves. Pelican Cove was apparently renowned for its surfing and today was no exception. There were numerous surfers out on the waves, their brightly coloured boards and shorts making them easy to pick out against the deep blue ocean.

Surfing. Another thing on the list of things she'd never tried. Maybe, once her baby was here, she would give it a go.

Lincoln pulled food from the basket and began setting it out on the blanket—chunky brown bread sandwiches, a pile of fruit and some sodas. He glanced around about them, acknowledging a few smiles and waves from people he recognised. People from the hospital at the beach with their families.

He'd only been here a few days and already people were recognising him. Was Pelican Cove really that small? Or was it just that friendly?

He watched as one of the nurses walked past, hand in hand with a chubby toddler. She gave him a small smile and joined her husband on a nearby blanket. Was that what they looked like? His head flicked from side to side. Did the other people on the beach assume that they were a family? He, Amy and the bump. Lincoln swallowed the lump currently fixed in his throat. That's what they must look like—walking down the coastal path hand in hand, like a husband and wife with a baby on the way. Lincoln felt uncomfortable.

What did he want people to think? Amy had already told people that she was his wife. No one had questioned her different surname. Did they know she'd been lying? Or were they just being polite, and not asking any questions? Even Val and Ruth, the two NICU nurses he'd brought with him from San Francisco's Children's Hospital—two nurses who had known him for the last five years—hadn't asked him about his *wife*. They knew he wasn't married. So why hadn't they asked any questions?

His eyes were drawn back to Amy. There was a smile on her face as she stared towards the ocean. Jennifer Taylor had been right about them being the same size. The outfit fitted perfectly, complementing her skin tone, even down to the wide-brimmed floppy hat.

The same question kept turning over and over in his mind. Why was Amy here? Was this just about her baby? Or had something else motivated her to come? Sure, he might be a good neonatologist, he might even be a great neonatologist, but there must have been someone else she worked with that she could have trusted—trusted with the life of her baby. Was it really just him? And was it really just his skills and expertise? Or was it something else, something deeper that had brought her here? And why, right now, was his stomach clenched in the hope that it was?

He blinked. Amy hadn't moved, her eyes still fixed on the horizon. 'What are you looking at?'

She smiled and turned towards him, leaning back on one of her elbows. 'The surfers. Something on my list.'

'Your list? What's that?'

She gave a little sigh. 'When I was sick I made myself a list of things I'd like to try once I was well again. It kind of helped me get through the bad days—the days when the chemo made me sick to my stomach and I thought I'd never get out of bed again.'

Lincoln felt a chill running down his spine. The thought she'd been *that* sick, *that* unwell really unnerved him. Why hadn't someone been there for her? Why hadn't *he* been there for her?

He forced a smile onto his face. 'So, surfing's on the list?' She nodded. 'What else?'

Amy leaned over and picked up one of the sandwiches he'd unpacked. She nibbled at a corner of it. 'There are lots of things. Lots of places I want to visit. Lots of things I want to experience that I haven't tried before.' Her hands ran over her stomach and her eyes met his. 'But there's one thing on the list that I've already got.'

He nodded. It was obvious that would be on the list. She'd had to undergo a cycle of fertility drugs to stimulate her ovaries before undergoing chemo so it kind of went without saying that having kids would be on the 'want to' list.

'Anything else I can help you with?'

She raised her eyebrow at him. 'You want to help with what's on the list?' She looked a little unsure.

Lincoln nodded. 'Why not?' Was it guilt that was making him say that? Guilt, because he hadn't been there for her when she'd been sick—even though she hadn't asked?

Amy shifted uncomfortably. 'I've never actually shown anyone my list,' she murmured.

Lincoln sat backwards. 'You actually have it—a list—written down?'

She nodded slowly, looking slightly amused. 'That's what a list is, Linc.'

This time as she watched him his smile reached his eyes, right up to the corners. Not like a few minutes ago. His eyes were twinkling. 'I thought we were talking hypothetical, I didn't realise you'd actually written it down.'

Amy bent forward and rummaged around her bag, unzipping a pocket inside and pulling out a piece of red paper, which she carefully unfolded and placed in the middle of the blanket. Lincoln leaned forward, intrigued. 'Silver pen?' He raised his eyebrows at her. 'Red and silver...' he nodded towards her feet '...just like your toes.'

Amy looked surprised and wriggled her toes in the sand. 'I hadn't even thought of that, and I was planning on changing my toes.' She wiggled them again. 'I like the stars but thought maybe midnight blue with gold stars this time.' She gave a little smile. 'More dramatic.' She waved her hand at the list. 'That's why I picked the red paper and silver pen, I wanted it to look bold, strong and powerful. Make me feel confident that I would be here to complete it.' Her voice had faded away and she was staring out at the ocean again.

Almost on instinct Lincoln reached out his hand and intertwined his fingers with hers. It was comfort, that was all. He was comforting a friend, showing support. So why did he feel the need to tell himself that inside his head?

He looked down at the paper again and gave her fingers

a squeeze. 'I think I would have to be a billionaire to help you with some of the things on this list.'

Amy looked embarrassed, pink tingeing her cheeks. 'Not all of them.' She leaned her head over next to his. 'Some of these were just wishful thinking.'

He quirked one eyebrow. 'That would be the two-carat diamond ring and the trip to Monte Carlo?'

She nodded. 'Exactly.' And took another bite of her sandwich. 'The others are much more reasonable.'

He looked at the neat, deliberate writing in front of him. Small script, carefully written.

1. Do whatever it takes to have a family.
2. Buy a gorgeous two-carat diamond ring.
3. Go on a trip to Monte Carlo and take a photograph outside the Hotel de Paris.
4. Learn to surf.
5. Learn to salsa.
6. Go to a *Star Trek* convention.
7. Travel on the cable cars in San Francisco.
8. Go back on the Amazon Aid Boat.
9. Join one of the social networking sites and find old friends.
10. Learn how to crochet and crochet a baby blanket.

A higgledy-piggledy, jumbled-up list. No priorities, just everything down there on paper.

The list looked a little well worn—rough around the edges—as if she'd pulled it from her bag on many occasions to read it. The red paper was still bright and the silver ink still glistened in the sun. It should be a happy, sunny list.

But it terrified him. Because for him it was evidence that at some point Amy had actually thought she was going to *die*. She'd actually put pen to paper and written a list of things she still wanted to do. She may have said the list was to make her feel better, but Linc was no fool. People didn't just write these lists to plan ahead—they wrote these lists as things to do before they *died*. And the thought made him feel physically sick. The sun was shining in the sky above him but the hairs on his arms were standing on end—as if he'd just walked through a chilly morgue.

He tried to push his thoughts away. He couldn't think about this. It was making him question everything about himself and his relationship with Amy. They'd been skirting around things. Playing at being friends—when they both knew there was a huge potential for more.

Did he want to have a relationship with Amy? Was it sensible? What if this pregnancy made her cancer come back? How would he feel then? And what about Amy's baby? Sure, he'd considered all the clinical aspects of a premature baby, but he hadn't considered the emotional aspects. The emotional aspects of having a relationship with a woman who had another man's baby. At least he had the satisfaction of knowing that the sperm donor would never appear. But that was little consolation if something happened to Amy. Would he be prepared to take on another man's child? Could he even consider bringing a baby up himself—one he had no genetic relationship with—if something happened to Amy?

Lincoln gave himself a shake. The sun was getting to him. He tried to focus on the list again and found his heart beating furiously in his chest. He looked at the items again. It couldn't be a coincidence—the boat and finding old friends. She'd produced a list when she'd been at her lowest ebb and two of the references on it could be about him.

Okay, so the list didn't say 'Find Lincoln Adams'. But

why would she want to go back to the Amazon aid boat? And why would she decide to look up old friends? Was it really all just some strange coincidence, or was he making a mountain out of a molehill?

He cleared his throat, readying himself to ask the obvious question. 'So how many of these have you actually done?'

Amy gave up on the sandwich and picked one of peaches he'd unpacked from the picnic basket, taking a big bite and letting the juice trickle down her chin. 'From the list?' He nodded. She was licking the juice from her fingers now. 'Just two.' Her voice sounded bright and breezy, as if she were discussing the latest episode of her favourite TV drama, instead of the 'try before you die' list.

He gave a little laugh. 'You're joking, right? Two? In five years?'

A wicked smile stole across her face. 'Let's just say I had a bit of a slow start,' she teased. Her hands rubbed her bump. 'And, anyway, this is a pretty big one. It's taken up a lot of my time.'

Lincoln leaned backwards. 'Okay, I'll give you that.' He watched as she discarded the half-eaten peach, wrapping it in a napkin and pulling out a lemon cupcake. 'Do you finish anything you eat these days?'

Amy peeled the case from the cupcake, tapping her stomach again. 'Not much room in here these days. I tend to eat little and often at the moment. I only really finish anything if it's the middle of the night—for some reason I'm always starving then.'

'So what was number two?'

'What?' Amy was lost in the land of lemon cupcake.

'You said you'd done two things on your list. Number one is obvious so what's number two?'

Amy waved her hand. 'Oh, that was easy. I made myself

a page on one of those social networking sites so I could track down some old friends.'

And with that wave of her hand Lincoln felt his insides plummet. She'd done the social networking, she'd tracked down 'old friends' and he obviously wasn't among them.

He shifted uncomfortably on the sand. 'Which one did you use?'

She named the most popular one around, one where he had a page posted.

He bit his bottom lip. 'So did you track down your old friends?'

Amy picked up a can of soda. 'Yeah, loads of them. All my old classmates from high school, old nursing friends from college, and people from some of the towns we stayed in as a kid—we moved about a lot.'

Lincoln asked the next question with a sinking feeling. 'So how many friends have you got, then?'

'Eight hundred and forty-two.' Eight hundred and forty-two. As if it were the easiest thing in the world. Pushing his paltry twenty-six 'friends' into oblivion. Amy changed position on the blanket. Moving up on to her knees and digging deep in the basket, she lifted her eyes, giving him an innocent smile. 'You know I reconnected with loads of people from the Amazon aid boat—Lily Carter, John Rhodes, Frank Kelly, Gene Hunt, Milly Johnson...' She finally found what she was looking for, a bunch of green grapes, and pulled them out from the basket. 'You know— you should join.'

For the first time in years Lincoln could feel the flush of colour in his cheeks. 'I've got a page,' he murmured.

'You have?' Her eyes were that bright, sparkly way again. 'You should send me a friend request, then—I'll accept.' A definite twinkle had appeared in her eye. She was teasing him again.

He rolled over on the blanket, groaning and putting his head in his hands. 'Okay, spill. How come you never sent me a friend request? You seem to have sent...' he waved his arms in front of him, out toward the ocean '...everyone else in the world one but me.'

Amy lay down next to him, resting her head in her hands, her hat flopping over her eyes. She was so close the length of her body was touching his, her bare legs next to his, the brim of her hat almost touching his head. She looked out toward the ocean, back at the surfers, and gave a little sigh.

'It just didn't feel right.'

His face was shadowed under her hat, his blue eyes even darker than normal. 'What do you mean, *it didn't feel right*?'

She looked downwards, towards the sand that was now trickling through her fingers. 'Some people knew that I'd been sick. They might have asked me how I was doing. I didn't want you to read it online.'

Lincoln opened his mouth and then stopped. It was time to use his head, not blurt out the first thing that came to mind. He pushed the thoughts of why she hadn't sent a private message to one side—along with the quip about whether it was more appropriate for her to turn up unannounced as his pregnant wife.

'I tried to find you, you know.' His fingers delved in the sand next to hers, pulling tiny pieces of a million years ago and rubbing them between his finger and thumb.

Her hand had stopped in mid-air. Her face turned to his. 'You did?' She looked shocked—surprised—as if it was the last thing she'd expected. Her green eyes were fixed on his, as if she was holding her breath, waiting for his response.

He moved his fingers from the sand and brushed them

off, putting his hand over hers. 'Of course I did.' He was looking directly at her. Something he hadn't done much in the last few days. Last time he'd looked at her like this had been when they'd kissed.

His finger touched her cheek. 'I'd just had the best six months of my life—professionally and personally—and then poof!' He blew into his fingers. 'The best thing disappeared.'

Amy could hear thudding in her ears. Was that the sound of her heart beating? Had he really just said that?

She felt a tingling sensation across her skin. Wasn't this what she'd really wanted to hear but he'd never said? She couldn't stop staring into those eyes. Those dark blue rims were really fascinating up close. Her throat felt dry, closed up, and she swallowed nervously. 'You never said anything,' she whispered. 'I thought I was just your summer fling.'

'I think six months qualifies as a little more than a summer fling.' He blinked, breaking off his gaze and staring back down at the sand. 'And, anyway, what was there to say?' His voice sounded rueful. 'I met a gorgeous girl and spent six fantastic months in bed with her, then she disappeared.' He never lifted his head, just kept staring at the sand, his hand scooping up big piles that he let run through his fingers again.

'I contacted a few people and tried to get your number, called Human Resources—who said that you'd quit. No one else on the boat seemed to have contact details for you. So that was it.'

So that was it. It sounded so final.

'You should have told me, Amy. You should have told me you were sick.' The sand was trickling through his fingers again. 'I don't think I can forgive the fact you didn't tell me.'

The words spun around in her head. After all this time, and all her explanations, he was still angry with her. The tiny spark that had been ignited inside her was dying. Being described as someone he'd 'spent six fantastic months in bed with' didn't fill her with inspiration. It made her feel like a sex object. Not a living, breathing human soul.

Not someone who he'd connected with. And definitely not someone he might have loved.

CHAPTER SIX

LINCOLN laid baby Esther on the scales again. Four pounds twelve ounces. A slight increase on her birth weight and she was finally feeding well. He gave Jennifer a little smile. 'Well, I think I can officially give the First Daughter a clean bill of health. There's really no reason to keep her here any longer.'

'I can go home?' The relief in Jennifer's eyes was apparent. Her husband, Charlie, had had to leave again two days ago and she was anxious to be with him.

Lincoln gave a nod.

'Do you have a preferred paediatrician in Washington? I'd like to handover to him or her before you go home.'

Jennifer gave a little nod. 'David Fairgreaves recommended someone to me—Linda Hylton. Have you heard of her?'

Lincoln nodded. 'We were paediatric residents together. She's great and she'll look after you. I know her number so I'll give her a call this afternoon.' He rolled his eyes at the black-suited figure visible through the glass in the door. 'I'll speak to your security detail. If you go home tomorrow, I'd expect you to see Linda in the next few days.' His nose wrinkled. 'I don't suppose you're going to be able to attend a regular appointment.' He shook his head, 'Obviously not. Once I've spoken to Linda, I'll give James

Turner her information and let him sort the appointment details out. Are you happy with that?'

Jennifer gave a watery smile. 'I'll just be happy to get home,' she whispered, then looked up again. 'Wait a minute—is Linda Hylton one of your love victims? Should I be careful what I say about you?'

Lincoln rolled his eyes. 'I don't know where you get these crazy ideas. I don't go out with *every* woman I meet.'

Jennifer folded her arms. 'So what was wrong with Linda Hylton?'

Lincoln smiled. 'Okay, you got me. She was dating one of my friends. Satisfied?'

Jennifer nodded her head, stifling her laugh.

'What about some help with your breastfeeding? Do you want me to arrange some support for you?'

Jennifer breathed a sigh of relief. 'Thankfully that's the one thing that I arranged a few months ago. I've got a friend who's a specialist NICU nurse in Washington—she's taking a leave of absence from her work for a few weeks and she's going to be around.'

Lincoln sat in the chair next to her, scribbling a few notes in the chart. 'Let me try and sort out the logistics of this.' He glanced around her jam-packed room, where even more presents seemed to have materialised. 'You just worry about how you're going to fit all this stuff into Air Force One.'

Jennifer shook her head. 'Now, now, Lincoln. It's only Air Force One if the President is on board—I thought everyone knew that. It's just an ordinary plane without him.'

Lincoln shook his head. 'I wouldn't let you fly with a neonate this young on an *ordinary* plane, Jennifer. But I'll do a final check on Esther before you go. Everything looks fine, so I don't imagine there will be any problems.'

Jennifer paused. 'Just out of interest, Linc. What does your "friend" make of your flirting?'

He stopped. The question had thrown him. He shrugged, shuffling the notes in his lap. 'Funnily enough, she's not interested in this hot body, she's only interested in my clinical skills.'

Something about saying those words made his stomach clench. He'd said them in jest but the irony wasn't lost on him. Amy had been clear about why she was here. For his skills as a neonatologist.

He went to stand up but Jennifer reached over and touched his arm. 'Did she like the maternity clothes?'

'Yes…yes, she did. Thank you. And you were right. They fitted perfectly.'

Jennifer gave a little nod, a little smile appearing on her face. 'I thought they might.' She waved her arms around the room. 'And your friend—does she need anything else? Anything for her baby?'

He shook his head. 'She's picked out most things and paid for them already. She just needs to pick them up.'

Then it struck him. Pick them up. From where? Suddenly it all seemed so ridiculous to him. How on earth was she going to be able to pick up her baby things?

He'd seen the baby catalogues stuffed in her bag and she'd showed him the items that she'd chosen. A white wooden baby crib and chest of drawers, a bright red pram and stroller, a zebra-print baby seat and a polished wooden high chair.

All apparently paid for and waiting in a store in Santa Maria, Butte County. Four hours away from where he stayed in San Francisco and even further from Pelican Cove.

'Thanks for all your help, Lincoln…' The First Lady was talking to him but his mind had drifted off. He was just about to discharge baby Esther, which meant that he, and his whole entourage of staff and equipment, should pack up and leave. Leave to go back to NICU at San Francisco Children's Hospital. Something that deep down he knew they all wanted to do.

But that would mean leaving Amy with no facilities for her baby. No staff and no equipment for a premature delivery. Her blood pressure was still borderline, with no particular response to the anti-hypertensives. She should be reviewed on a daily basis. Who would do that if they all left?

'So I was wondering if you would mind?'

'Mind? Mind what?' Lincoln snapped out of his thoughts with the distinct impression he'd just missed something important.

Jennifer laughed, the amused expression on her face unhidden. 'You haven't listened to a single word I said—have you?'

Lincoln felt embarrassed.

'You're too busy thinking about a beautiful redhead, I imagine.'

'What? No? Of course not.' He was babbling and he knew it.

'Oh, don't make excuses, Linc, you've done everything you can for me...' she bent her head and kissed her baby on the forehead '...and Esther.' She waved her hand in the air. 'So go and see your lady friend.'

Lincoln's lips formed a tight smile and he left the room, stopping in the middle of the corridor. What on earth was he going to do? He'd promised to look after Amy's baby—how could he do that in San Francisco?

He strode quickly down the corridor. Right now he needed someone to talk to. Someone who could give him some advice. But all his friends were in San Francisco, and the only other people he knew well were Val and Ruth. He couldn't discuss Amy with them, it just wasn't his style.

He walked out the front doors of the hospital into the Californian sunshine. It was another gorgeous day. Just like the one a few days ago when he'd taken Amy for the picnic on the beach.

The day that had left an awkward and uncomfortable silence between them. He'd obviously said something to offend her—but, for the life of him, he couldn't think what it was. She seemed almost…disappointed in him.

Lincoln walked over to one of the benches outside the hospital doors and sat down. He took a long, slow breath, in and out. He had to take some time to think about this—think about what to do.

If he discharged baby Esther tomorrow, he would have to tell Amy that it was time for his staff and equipment to leave Pelican Cove. So why did his stomach churn at the mere thought of that?

He stared out over the ocean, watching the crashing waves. It was time to stop skirting around the edges. It was time to face up to the facts. How did 'playboy Linc' really feel about Amy?

He could remember how much he'd missed her when she'd left the boat. But then he'd thought it was only a holiday and she'd be back before he knew it. Except she hadn't been.

When she'd gone on holiday it had hit him how much he missed her. He'd lain awake in his cabin at night, listening to the sounds of the Amazon rain forest, his thoughts filled with her, stealing his sleep away from him. He'd watched the calendar hanging in the galley, counting the days until she came back.

Except she hadn't.

And the feelings that had descended on him when she

hadn't returned had been a first for him. He had been frustrated beyond belief by the fact that no one had been able to tell him where she was, or why she hadn't returned. Most of the other staff had just shrugged their shoulders and said it happened often—people went home to their nice, clean homes and calm lives, and decided not to return to the damp, humid conditions of the Amazon.

Everyone just seemed to accept it and carry on with their lives—whilst Lincoln had felt as if he was losing his mind.

So he'd pushed it all away. Put his mind on the job at hand, the fate of a thousand people living on the banks of the Amazon and coming for medical care and treatment. Then, six months later, his new position in the States at San Francisco's Children's Hospital and the chance to be part of a world-class team had arisen.

But he couldn't shake her from her his mind. He couldn't replace her in his thoughts with the next nurse that came along—the next woman who showed interest in him. Even his potential bride didn't push her from his thoughts. Poor Polly didn't deserve the cold way he had treated her, but in the end he just couldn't stop the visions of the long red curly hair and dark green eyes.

Even months later, in another world, another city, he would see a turn of a head, a flash in the corner of his eye and the feeling of his heart in his mouth when he'd thought he'd glimpsed her again, only to have it plummet seconds later at the realisation it wasn't her. It wasn't Amy.

And then, a few days ago, he'd seen her again and all those feelings came rushing back. His skin on fire, his heart pounding in his chest, and the sick feeling in his stomach when he realised she was unwell, and then again when he realised she was pregnant.

The horror when she told him she'd been ill. Breast

cancer. Even now, the mere thought of it made him angry. Those tiny malicious cells growing around her body, filling her with disease. Filling her with fear for her future. Then the horror of her treatment—treatment that some people maintained was worse than the disease. How on earth had she managed that on her own?

He shook his head. How would he have coped if it had been him? Could he have been so brave? So sure? So steadfast? So determined? Then the list—the list she'd written to get her through. To give her focus and a way ahead.

Another sensation surrounded him and he sank his head into his hands. Because this feeling made him feel sick to the pit of his stomach. Guilt.

Guilt about the relief he'd felt when she'd revealed that there was no one in her life. No husband. No father for the baby.

Was that wrong of him? Was it wrong of him to feel that way? Was it wrong that those words had given him a small sliver of hope?

And what about the baby? If Amy's condition didn't improve, her baby could arrive in a matter of a few weeks, or even days. Would that change the way he felt about her? He was a playboy, no matter how much he detested the word. He'd never given children a second thought—well, not children of his own.

His stomach was churning. Any day now he was going to have to pack up and leave. But what would happen to Amy then?

She could stay here in Pelican Cove. David would continue to be her obstetrician. But there was no neonatologist if she had an early delivery. It was routine procedure that any woman at risk in Pelican Cove would be transferred to San Francisco. His home. Chances were, he would have ended up being her neonatologist by default if she'd turned up there.

This was so complicated. Should he offer her help? Support? What would he do if this was just another female friend? If this wasn't Amy—a woman who messed with his mind just by being there?

The most sensible solution was to invite her to stay with him in San Francisco and let her continue her obstetric care there until the baby arrived. That's what he would do for anyone else. Anyone he considered a friend.

The thoughts jumbled around in his head. But was that really sensible? She could deliver in two days or two weeks. How would it feel to have Amy in his apartment— under his roof?

Lincoln closed his eyes and took a deep breath. He was helping a friend. And maybe, just maybe, if he kept repeating that, he might actually believe it.

Lincoln stood at the nurses' station and looked over Amy's chart quickly. David had reviewed her again this morning, taken more blood samples and adjusted her blood-pressure meds.

The handwritten script in the case notes was precise. David felt she was teetering at the edge. She was still clearly at risk of her pre-eclampsia developing into the full blown disease. He wanted her treated with caution and monitored daily.

Lincoln understood. And strangely it filled him with confidence that he'd made the right decision and was about to take the right steps.

He leaned over to the nearest computer and checked his e-mail account. Because he was away from his normal hospital, all his e-mails were currently being diverted to his personal account. 'What the…?' He leaned in closer to his account. Three thousand e-mails. He squinted at the screen. A voice behind him laughed, leaning over his shoulders.

'Wow,' she said, 'that's a *lot* of friend requests.'

Lincoln shook his head, 'I don't get it,' he mumbled, the thoughts of his paltry list of twenty-six friends the day before bewildering him. 'Who on earth are all these people?' His eyes ran up and down the names on the list. 'I don't even recognise any of them.'

The nurse behind him patted him on the shoulder. 'That's what happens when you appear on the TV as the President's doctor, handsome.' She gave a little laugh as she walked away.

Lincoln sat for a few seconds. Instant fame. He hadn't even given it much thought. One television appearance and suddenly half the world wanted to be his 'friend'.

A small hand positioned itself on the box on the counter next to him. 'Lincoln, we didn't know you cared.'

His hands shot out and grabbed the cake box and carton of coffee on the counter. 'I don't.' He gave the nurse a smile. 'Hands off. These are my bargaining tools and I think I'm going to need them.'

She shook her head. 'Just don't let her throw them off the wall—those cupcakes are too good to waste.'

Amy's door was slightly ajar and he could see her lying in the darkened room. Her blinds were drawn to block out the glaring sun and she lay on her side on the bed, her eyes closed, wearing a pale blue smock and drawstring linen trousers.

'Knock, knock.'

Her eyelids flickered open, a smile starting on her face before her brain switched into gear and she remembered she was angry with him.

She pushed herself up the bed. 'Hi, Lincoln, what do you want?'

He put his gifts on the bedside table, pushing it up towards her until it sat just before her extended abdomen.

Amy took a deep breath. Coffee. That was definitely coffee she could smell. She lifted the lid on the cup and inhaled. Even better, it was a caramel latte. She'd seriously thought about killing someone for one of these the other day.

She pulled the pink ribbon on the cake box, tugging it clear and lifting the lid on the box. Cupcakes. Strawberry, chocolate and lemon. And all of them had her name written on them. Literally.

Her taste buds started watering. Lincoln knew her well. The best way to her heart was through her stomach. What was he up to?

She picked up a pink cupcake, peeled the paper case and took a bite. 'Mmm. I know that there is probably an ulterior motive to these…' she raised her hand '…but I don't want you to tell me what it is until I've finished eating. I *don't* want you to spoil this.' She eyed the cup. 'I thought you weren't letting me drink coffee?'

'It's a special occasion.'

She took a sip of the caramel latte. Perfect. Her taste buds exploded. Oh, how she'd missed this. Her eyes swept over the box of cakes. Could she eat another before he started speaking? Probably. They were tiny—two bites and they were gone. Her fingers hovered over a chocolate cupcake, the next in the box.

She lifted her eyes to look at him. Lincoln was sitting in the chair next to her bed, waiting patiently for her to finish. But he didn't look ill at ease or nervous. No, he looked cool, calm and confident. In short, he didn't look like a man who thought he'd have to bribe his way into the room. He looked like a man who'd already made whatever decision had to be made. And it made her feel distinctly uncomfortable.

She set down the chocolate cupcake, praying whatever he said wasn't about to ruin her appetite. 'What do you want, Linc?'

He nodded slowly, his eyes fixing on hers. 'We need to talk, Amy.'

She bit her lip. Where was this going to go? 'What about?'

He sat a little straighter. 'Baby Esther is ready to go home—to go back to the White House. She's ready for discharge, and once I finish her paperwork, the plans will be in place.'

Amy nodded. What did this have to do with her?

Lincoln's face was serious. 'Once she's ready to go, *I* have to go. *We* have to go.'

The penny dropped. Like a huge boulder throwing itself off the edge of a cliff. 'Oh.'

She should have known this was coming. At first, it hadn't even occurred to her—the fact that Lincoln wouldn't be staying here. She'd been so caught up in getting to where he was and making him agree to look after her baby that she'd had tunnel vision. But after a few days stuck as an inpatient in Pelican Cove she'd started to worry. The First Lady wasn't likely to stay here for long. What would happen then? The truth was, she'd more or less expected to have her baby in a matter of days. But Junior seemed to be making his own plans.

'So, it's time to make a decision.' Amy felt as if she could throw up. Once baby Esther left, there was no reason for any of the staff or facilities that had been spirited into Pelican Cove to stay. What about her? What about her baby? And why did Lincoln look so calm?

'I need to pack up all the NICU equipment and arrange for my staff to return to San Francisco.'

Duh. She'd just realised that.

'I need to return to San Francisco, as I've got duties and commitments there…'

She nodded dumbly. Of course he did.

'So I thought it best to make some arrangements for you and the baby.' He picked up her chart. She hadn't even noticed him bringing it into the room. *Arrangements*. Did he know how clinical that sounded?

'David still has some concerns about your condition. You're coming up on twenty-nine weeks, but your blood pressure is still borderline—even with the anti-hypertensives—and you're still showing protein in your urine.'

His hand brushed against hers, his voice softening, becoming less businesslike and more friendlike. 'Chances are, this baby is still going to come early. You came to Pelican Cove because you wanted me to be the one to look after your baby. Is that still what you want, Amy?'

She nodded. Words escaped her right now. Her mind was too full of jumbled thoughts to say anything coherent. Where was this going?

Lincoln nodded and gave her a little smile. 'In that case, I think I might have found a solution for us, then.'

'Solution?' The word gave her hope. Because, right now, she needed some.

'You can come back to San Francisco with me.' There. He'd said it. The words that had been coiled up inside his chest since he'd came to the conclusion a few hours ago. In his head, that made perfect sense.

Right now he was leaving out the way he felt drawn to her room in the hospital, day or night, for no good reason. She was like a magnet to him and he was instantly drawn.

And in his head that was perfect. She'd disappeared out

of his life before and he'd no intention of letting it happen again. But this time he'd be more careful. Amy had searched him out. She'd come to find him. She wanted his skills and expertise—and she could have them. And maybe it could give him some time to work out how he felt about her.

It took him a few seconds to realise she hadn't spoken. She seemed frozen to the spot, or to the bed. Her mouth was hanging open, and her hands had the slightest tremor.

Time to fill in the blanks. Time to persuade her it was most reasonable and viable option for her.

'I know you've been looked after in Santa Maria—but you came here because you didn't have a physician there you could trust. And the most important thing is that you have someone you trust looking after your baby.

'David will be staying in Pelican Cove. He could continue to treat you, if that's what you prefer. But even he is worried about an early delivery. The normal protocol in Pelican Cove is that someone in your condition would be transferred to San Francisco Children and Maternity Hospital—where we have excellent facilities for neonates.'

He let her take in the words, rationalise it in her brain.

'I can arrange for one of the obstetricians there to take over your care. There are two I would absolutely trust with my life. I wouldn't recommend them to you otherwise.'

He ran his fingers through his tousled hair, a sign of his nerves. Was this going well?

'We could arrange to get there tomorrow. I'll get one of the obstetricians to review you immediately and decide on how to proceed. If there's any emergency, I'll be close by and available to be at the delivery.'

His words hung in the air. There. He'd said them. And whilst he knew every word he'd said was true, there was still that tiny little bit of him that knew there was an element of emotional blackmail in there. He was using her fear for her child to get her exactly where he wanted her.

He didn't like the word *manipulate*. It seemed like something from a bad-guy movie. Something that the villain did. But he'd never said he was perfect. He'd never said he didn't have flaws. He was just a man. Trying to get his girl.

Amy's hands were resting on the bedside table— probably to control a tremor. She thought of her empty apartment in Santa Maria, with the baby's things still flat-packed into boxes. She didn't have any family any more, but she had good friends there who were happy to help out and support her. She was lucky that she had regular hours at the clinic that meant she could plan her childcare hours in advance. So why did it feel as if all the plans she had made were crumbling around her?

'But where would I stay? I don't know anyone in San Francisco?' It looked as if it was just one of a million thoughts that were currently scurrying around in her brain.

'That's easy. You'll stay with me.'

Amy choked, then coughed and spluttered, her face turning redder and redder by the second. Lincoln jumped to his feet and leapt behind her, thumping his hand on her back until she stopped then grabbing a glass of water from the nearby locker and handing it to her. 'Here, take this.'

She took a little sip, taking in deep frantic breaths, try-ing to fill her lungs with the air that seemed to have been sucked from them when he'd said those words.

She blew the air out slowly through thick pursed lips, then turned to face him. 'How on earth can I come and stay with you, Lincoln? You haven't seen me in six years. You don't owe me anything. Yes, I want you to deliver my baby but I don't expect anything else from you, and I cer-tainly don't expect *this*.'

Her voice was slow and steady, but he could see the panic in her eyes. She was frantic, swimming in an ocean where she was out her depth and being pulled out with the current. Seemed she was as scared of the scenario as he was.

'Amy, the fact is you can stay anywhere you want to. But if you are going to come to San Francisco, it makes sense that you stay with a friend. There's no point in running up a hotel bill—you could deliver tomorrow, or in six weeks' time. And in your current condition it makes even more sense if that friend has some medical expertise.' The words were plain. Sensible, and he knew it. They sounded rational and reasonable.

They didn't tell her that his heart was suddenly thudding against his chest and his stomach was turning inside out at the thought of her not agreeing to this.

'I'd like to think that as soon as we get to San Francisco one of my colleagues will assess you. They might even want to admit you. But if, like Pelican Cove, they want to see you on a daily basis, it makes sense that you stay with me. I live five minutes away from the hospital in a two-bedroom apartment. I've got a housekeeper that comes in twice a week, so you won't feel obliged to do anything. Just relax with your feet up and wait for this baby to arrive.'

She was still silent. It looked as if she were trying to formulate words in her brain. Was she looking for an easy way to let him down? To tell him she couldn't possibly stay with him? He couldn't hear that.

It was time to play his trump card.

He kept his voice strong and confident. He wanted her to feel assured, safe. He also wanted to play to her fun side. 'Look at it this way, Amy, you'll get to do another thing on your list.'

'My list?' Her eyes were blank, as if the list was the last thing on her mind.

Lincoln nodded and touched her hand. 'I didn't mention where I stay, did I? I've got an apartment in Fisherman's Wharf in San Francisco. It's actually just where the cable cars turn to start their journey again. You'll have number seven on your list at your fingertips.'

Even as he said the words he questioned his wisdom. Doing something on her list was never going to be the deciding factor for her. But right now desperate times called for desperate measures. And he'd use whatever it took.

She looked a bit dazed, shocked.

'Amy?'

Her voice had the slightest tremor. 'It's a lot to think about.' She stood up and pushed the bedside table away, walking over to the window and looking out over Pelican Cove. Her hands were placed protectively over her stomach, as if she were cradling her baby inside.

Inside her brain was in turmoil. Why hadn't she planned ahead? Why hadn't she foreseen this? The safety of her baby was always going to be paramount, but what about the safety of her soul?

The last few days had brought a huge surge of emotions to the fore. Maybe they were pregnancy related? But right now every time she was in a room with Lincoln she couldn't think of anything else.

The thought of running up a hotel bill made her blood run cold. Her maternity salary was comfortable enough to cover her rent and outgoings, but not unexpected outgoings like these.

Stay in his apartment? He must be out of his mind! She had visions in her head of two lions stalking around their prey. That's what it would feel like. How could she possibly be relaxed around Lincoln when every second she would be waiting to see if he would touch her, look at her, take her in his arms and…

'I don't think it would work.' The words were out before she had a chance to think about them.

'Why?' Lincoln looked confused. He walked towards her and put his arms on either side of her shoulders. His face seemed so open, so honest. With no concerns, no worries. He really didn't know. He really didn't realise what he did to her.

But, then, how could he, if she'd never told him?

'I… I…' Her throat was dry, her tongue sticking to the top of her mouth.

'It's the perfect solution—surely you can see that?' Then he did it. He gave her that killer smile. The one that used to unnerve her from across the room and make her knees buckle. The smile that sent a thousand feather-like touches skittering across her skin. And something inside her heart lurched.

Hope. The feeling she'd felt when she'd seen him on television and had known she'd be able to find him and ask for help.

The sensations that had engulfed her when she'd first set eyes on him after six long years.

The heat and warmth that had swept through her body when he'd touched her, when he'd kissed her.

The look in his eyes on the beach when he'd told her that he'd searched for her and it had sent loose a thousand butterflies, beating their wings inside her chest.

Hope.

A sensation she only recognised now. The same sensation she'd steeled inside herself when she'd written the list.

He reached up, catching a curl of hair that had fallen in front of her eye, tucking it behind her ear. He was looking at her with those dark-rimmed eyes. She was mesmerised. And she wanted more.

Maybe this was the way to get it.

'You're right,' she breathed. 'It makes perfect sense. When do we leave?'

CHAPTER SEVEN

Amy looked out of the apartment window, across the rippling San Francisco bay to Alcatraz. What a view. It was strange how a piece of rock could seem so foreboding and enigmatic, rising up from the grey waves. Even from this distance she could see the ferry pulling in again, no doubt unloading its cargo of tourists all anxious to capture the moment on camera.

Everywhere she looked there were tourists. The iconic Powell-Hyde cable car turntable at Fisherman's Wharf was practically under her nose, with a constant stream of people lining up to get their photo snapped next to it. She looked back over her shoulder, into the spacious wooden-floored apartment. This really was a prime piece of real estate and she shuddered to think how much it had cost.

Amy glanced at her watch for the third time in ten minutes. 'Resting' wasn't easy for a girl who was used to being on her feet in a busy ward for twelve hours a day. Three long days she'd been looking out of this window into the wonderful world of bustling San Francisco beneath her. Currently just out of her reach.

Daily hospital monitoring and strict bed rest. It almost sounded like a prison sentence. The irony of the view of Alcatraz wasn't lost on her.

Her blood pressure hadn't improved, her urine still had

protein in it, but thankfully her oedema was under control and she hadn't developed any other symptoms. It hadn't stopped her newest obstetrician, Cassidy Yates—a statuesque blonde who watched Lincoln out of the corner of her eye—from referring to the local protocols and administering some steroids to help develop the baby's lungs in case of early delivery. For the past three days Amy had travelled with him into work and he'd dropped her at the day unit for monitoring and assessment.

Twenty-nine weeks and three days. Right now her extended abdomen felt like a ticking time bomb. Then there was being *here*. In Lincoln's apartment, surrounded all day by little pieces of him.

The good thing was…he'd been the perfect gent. Welcoming, considerate and ever attentive. The frustrating thing was…he'd been the perfect gent. And it was driving her crazy.

Amy sighed and flopped down into the nearby red leather armchair, pushing until the seat tilted backwards and the leg rest sprang out. There was nothing to do— Lincoln had said he would take care of dinner, so all she could do right now was wait.

The trouble with waiting was that it left too much time to think. Too much time to look out at the busy life below and wonder when you could be part of it again. She felt a sharp kick under her ribs and drew a deep breath. She pulled up her smock top to reveal her baby bump.

She watched the squirms under her skin—if this were a movie, any minute now a twelve-armed alien would burst from her stomach. Baby Zachary had obviously decided to have a party in there, and he was certainly beginning to object to the reducing space. Her hands hovered just above her belly, wondering where the next punch would appear. It really was amazing to think that she would hold him in her arms soon. What would he look like? Would he have red hair and pale skin like her? Or the physical characteristics of his sperm donor father?

She could remember the details on the resume. Sperm Donor 867. Dark hair, green eyes (best to choose someone with the same eye colour you had), over six feet tall, college education. But did any of that really matter? Would genetics really decide the sum of her baby? Was it all nature or was it nurture?

She lifted her hands to her head, gently massaging her temples. Her head was starting to throb slightly, nothing to worry about—not enough to search the cupboards for paracetamol, just enough to annoy her thought processes.

What would her son's interests be? Her sperm donor had been a jock—no doubt about that. Every sport known to man had been on his list of interests. What did she know about football? But he'd also been academic, and had specialised in education.

So would her son be like his father or more like her? Reckless at times, occasionally unpredictable? In future years would she have to sit up at night, worrying about what time he would come in?

Zachary squirmed again under her skin, as if sensing her breath was currently caught in her chest. Why did she feel so panicked? She'd started this process six years ago—more than enough time to think about the end product. She'd spent the last two weeks worrying about premature birth and safe delivery. So why now was she panicking about hair colour and little-boy interests?

'That's some sight.'

Amy let out a shriek, pulling down her smock top and leaping up from the chair. Lincoln stood leaning against the doorframe, his arms folded across his chest, a smile of amusement on his face.

'Lincoln! I didn't hear you.' She could feel the colour rushing into her face. 'Where did you spring from?'

He crossed the room in a couple of steps, his hands resting lightly on the tops of her arms. 'Where I always spring from—work. Sorry, didn't mean to scare you.'

'You didn't… Well, you did, but I think that I… I mean…'

'You're babbling.' His voice was calm, but there was a distinct twinkle in his eye that even she could notice in the dimming light.

She looked around her. When had it got so dark? 'What time is it?'

'Just after seven. Sorry I'm a bit late, we had an emergency in NICU.'

She gave a quiet nod—she could hardly object, conscious of the fact that in a few days' or weeks' time her baby could be the emergency in NICU.

'I guess I lost track of time,' she murmured looking back out over the bustling city. Last time she'd looked outside it had been late afternoon. Had she drifted off to sleep? Her stomach growled loudly, reminding her of why she'd been waiting for Linc. 'Did you bring dinner?'

'Ahh…about that…' His forehead puckered in a frown.

This time it was her turn to smile. 'You forgot—didn't you?'

'Not exactly.' He extended his arm towards her, trying to push aside the delicious thoughts of the scene he'd just witnessed, his brain swiftly improvising. 'I decided to take you out to dinner. You must be going crazy, stuck in my apartment.'

Amy pressed her palms against the window. 'I don't know if crazy is the right word, but I definitely feel as if I'm missing out on something. I've dreamed about exploring San Francisco for years, and now that I'm here I feel as if it's just outside my reach.' She turned to face him and flattened her back against his picture window. 'I want to ride on the cable cars—I don't want to watch them turn underneath me. I want to do the boat trip to Alcatraz and stand in the cells and feel the atmosphere of the place. I want to go down to Pier 39 and have my picture taken next to the Fisherman's Wharf sign. I want to go and explore Chinatown. I want to eat there, see the colours and smell all the wonderful food. I want to spend the day wandering around Fisherman's Wharf wondering what type of ice cream I want to eat next. I want to sit in some of the quayside restaurants and eat all the fish on the menu.'

Lincoln raised his eyebrow at her, folding his arms across his chest. 'You have been going crazy in here, haven't you? Why didn't you say something sooner?'

She sighed. 'You've been busy, Linc. The last thing you need to do is try and entertain an uninvited house guest.'

He shook his head. 'Why do you keep saying stuff like that?'

'Stuff like what?'

His brow was puckered again. '*Uninvited* house guest.' He looked annoyed. 'You're not uninvited. I invited you.' He swung his arms wide, 'This is my home. I wanted you here.'

Amy licked her lips, as if she was preparing to say something. Her eyes were fixed on his again. And he could sense something. Something bubbling just underneath the surface, getting ready to erupt. The hairs stood up at the back of his neck, making him feel distinctly uncomfortable. All of sudden he felt as the though the walls of his spacious apartment were starting to close in around him.

'Come on.' He extended his arm towards her, anxious to break the tension between them. 'You can pick wherever you like. Let's eat.'

* * *

The street was packed. The early evening tourists were crammed onto the sidewalks, reading menus and deciding what restaurant to eat in. Lincoln weaved seamlessly through the crowd and pushed open a heavy wooden door, holding it open until Amy was safely inside.

She blinked furiously, her eyes struggling to adjust to the gloomy interior, but Lincoln took her hand again and eased her through the dimly lit restaurant, pulling her into a wooden seated booth.

'I thought I was getting to pick?'

He rolled his eyes. 'If we'd waited for you to pick, we'd still be standing on the sidewalk at midnight, peering at menus.'

He handed her a plastic-coated menu. 'What do you want to eat?'

Amy looked around her. The gaudily decorated interior of fake wooden barrels and ship's wheels draped with Hawaiian garlands left her speechless. To say nothing of the life-size pirate standing the corner of the room.

'This looks like a bit of a tourist trap,' she mumbled, her eyes running over the menu in the hope it could redeem itself to her.

Lincoln leaned back in the booth, 'That's the beauty of this place,' he said, a smile plastered across his face. 'It looks dark and seedy. But it hides San Francisco's best-kept secret. My mate Johnny is the chef and he makes the best food in the world.' He leaned across the booth towards her. 'So what do you fancy?'

The English terminology made her blink, as did the double meaning. What she 'fancied' wasn't on the menu in front of her. But right now she couldn't even contemplate what she 'fancied'. Not while she currently felt like a beached whale.

Her tongue ran nervously along her lips, her eyes fixed

on the plastic menu—because looking upwards would mean staring into those deep blue eyes and she couldn't face that right now. Junior gave another kick and she winced.

Lincoln's hand shot across the table and caught hers. 'Are you okay? Is something wrong?'

Yes, yes, something was wrong. Her brain couldn't focus. Her rational thoughts had left the building. She wanted to blurt out everything that was currently spinning around in her head. She wanted to tell him that she wished she'd called him six years ago when she'd got the cancer diagnosis. She wanted to tell him that she wished the baby she was currently carrying in her belly was his, instead of donor 867's. She wanted to tell him that she wished she'd had her surgery and her body looked normal again so she could finally stand and look at her naked reflection in the mirror again. She wanted to tell him that her back ached, her feet were sore and her headache was really starting to annoy her—but he'd just taken her out and the last thing she wanted to do right now was head back to the apartment. Because there it would just be the two of them. Alone.

Suddenly the grubby-looking restaurant didn't seem so bad. At least there were other people around.

A man appeared and slapped Lincoln on the shoulder. 'Who's the lovely lady, Linc? And why haven't you introduced me?'

Lincoln smiled. He seemed relaxed and easy in here and the tension that had been between them seemed to have left his tightened shoulders. He held his hand out towards Amy. 'This, Johnny, is my good friend Amy Carson. She's never sampled the delights of your cooking, so I hope you're going to impress her—otherwise she'll bend my ear all night for bringing her to such a dive.' He gave her a little wink across the table.

Johnny laughed. A deep, hearty laugh that seemed to come from all the way down at his toes. 'Impress? Me? Once I've fed this lady, she'll never look at you again, Linc.' He bent his head and picked up Amy's hand, kissing it with a flourish. 'So, beautiful, what can I get you?'

Amy looked back at Linc in panic. She hadn't even read the menu properly yet.

Lincoln pointed towards her. 'Why don't you decide for us, Johnny? Only be careful what you give my pregnant friend, we're hoping to avoid an early labour.'

Johnny's eyes turned to where Amy's extended abdomen was tucked neatly under the table in the darkened booth. He beamed. 'Congratulations, beautiful lady. I'm sure I can rustle something up that will delight your little bambino.'

He wandered back off to the kitchen and left the two of them sitting in the booth. Amy held her breath. Johnny was obviously a friend; would he assume the baby was Lincoln's? Or was her imagination just making wild leaps?

She could be a colleague from work, a neighbour, an old friend from school. There was no reason for Johnny to think anything else. So why was half of her hoping that he was?

Her stomach growled loudly. 'So what am I going to get to eat, Linc? With my current busy lifestyle, food is becoming a very important part of my day.'

Lincoln smiled at the lilt in her voice. This was the Amy he remembered. A bit cheeky, with a definite sarcastic edge. Not the nervous and uptight woman he'd spent the last few days with.

'I think I can safely say you'll get a feast fit for a king.'

'Or a queen?' The teasing tone was apparent.

'Ouch. Yes, or a queen.' He rested his head on his hands. 'What did Cassidy say today?'

Amy could feel the smile drop from her face. Why was it the mere mention of that woman's name automatically put her hackles up? Cassidy had only ever been pleasant and professional to Amy, but Amy could see the way Cassidy looked at Lincoln—even if he couldn't. His easy flirtatious manner was coming back to bite him on the...

'Nothing's changed. I've to go back tomorrow for more of the same.'

Lincoln leaned back and looked at her face. She looked vaguely irritated, as if she was annoyed. Surely, at this stage, no news was good news?

'So what's with the long face?'

Amy took a deep breath. This was where she should play the nice house guest. Happy, amenable and anxious to please.

Except these pregnancy hormones were driving her nuts. Her aching back was driving her nuts. Living under the same roof as Lincoln was driving her nuts. And seeing some gorgeous, statuesque blonde looking at Lincoln, *her Lincoln*, the way that woman did was driving her nuts.

She opened her mouth to speak just as Johnny reappeared and slid the biggest platter known to man onto their table. Grilled shrimp, Dungeness crab, scallops and crab cakes with rice and salad on the side. Then another plateful with grilled chicken, peppers, onion, a bowl of ratatouille and some garlic bread. Johnny folded his arms across his chest. 'Before you start, I know all of this is high in Omega 3 and can assure you it's all completely fresh and fully cooked. No tuna, no tilefish, no mackerel. All safe for a pregnant lady.' He shrugged his shoulders. 'But I also made you some chicken and garlic bread in case you were a little wary.'

Amy's face relaxed as the wonderful smell of freshly cooked fish wafted towards her. Her smile lit up her face. 'Johnny, how can a girl come to Fisherman's Wharf and not sample the Dungeness crab?'

She lifted her napkin from the table and spread it across her bump. 'Not the most glamorous, I know, but I'd hate to ruin these gorgeous clothes that you stole for me from the First Lady.'

Lincoln laughed as he pulled a plate towards him and started lifting some food from the platter. The maternity clothes had been a godsend. Today Amy was wearing a deep purple smock, which complemented her red hair and pale skin perfectly. In fact, every time he saw her she had a different outfit on. He had the distinct impression that the First Lady had known exactly the impact her 'cast-off' clothes would have. Brownie points. Big time. 'I didn't steal them. She wanted you to have them. And it's obvious you're making good use of them—that's what she wanted.'

Amy lifted a fork to her mouth. 'So are you going to tell me anything interesting about the First Lady?'

'And break patient confidentiality?' He'd raised one eyebrow at her, in mock indignation, then bent over and took a bite of his crab, shaking his head as he quickly swallowed. 'Nope. I'm not going to tell you a thing. Except she wanted you to use those clothes. Oh, and that she called me an incorrigible flirt—how dare she?'

Amy laughed. 'Well, she got that right.'

'I do not flirt, I'm just a friendly person,' Lincoln protested.

Amy rolled her eyes. 'Women fall at your feet everywhere, Linc.'

He paused for a second, as if lost in a thought, 'Mmm, not all women. It's only useful if it's the woman you want.'

The air seemed to go silent around them. Amy bit her

lip. *What did that mean*? Did he mean her? Had she fallen at his feet on the Amazon boat and he hadn't wanted her to? Or was he talking about now, and how she was trying to keep her distance? She had no idea what was going on inside his head.

Amy took another bite of her shrimp, then broke the garlic bread in half, handing it to him across the table. A little twinge came across her back. Junior felt as if he was turning around inside her right now. She crossed then uncrossed her ankles, trying to find a more comfortable position.

'Everything okay?'

'That's twice you've asked in the last fifteen minutes.'

'And that's twice I've caught you looking at me as if you want to take a meat cleaver to my head.' Lincoln put his food back on the plate. 'So spill, Amy, what's eating you?'

'Nothing.'

Lincoln gave a sigh and lifted his glass of root beer, which had magically appeared at his side. 'So, if nothing's wrong, quit being snarky. I've had a crappy day at work and I just want to come home and relax.'

'Snarky? Is that even a word?' She couldn't help it. No matter how hard she tried, the words were practically a growl.

He lifted one eyebrow at her again. It was a habit of his that was really beginning to annoy her. No matter how chilled she tried to be.

'Amy, I'm only going to ask this once more. What's wrong?'

All of a sudden the gorgeous platter of food didn't seem so appetising. It looked as if it could catch in her throat and choke her to death. Worse, she could feel tears start to form in her eyes. Why was she about to cry? What the hell was wrong with her?

She gulped as one tear escaped and slid down her cheek and she fumbled for her napkin. 'Nothing's wrong. And everything's wrong. That's just it, Linc. I don't know what's wrong—I just know something is.'

Within seconds he'd reached across the table and captured her hands in his. She could feel the warmth from his hands creeping up her arms. Her hands felt cold, like blocks of ice. Truth be told, her whole body felt like that.

Another tear slid down her face and she pulled her hand away, brushing the paper napkin against her face. 'Damn pregnancy hormones,' she muttered.

'Don't, Amy. Don't do that. Don't blame this on the fact you're pregnant. We both know it's not that.' His voice cut through the dim light like a brilliant strobe, making her breath catch in her throat. He was looking directly at her, one hand now at the back of his head, pulling at his hair. His frustration was evident.

Silence. She didn't know what to say. She didn't know what she should say. She didn't know what she *could* say.

In her head it was easy. She was a princess in a pink satin dress, standing at the top of her tower, and he was Prince Charming on the white charger below. But she wasn't a child, and this wasn't a fairy-tale. This was real and in her head the princess wasn't pregnant with a sperm donor's baby and hadn't suffered from breast cancer and had a mastectomy. In her head the princess was the perfect healthy, whole, fertile partner that Prince Charming deserved.

Something she would never be.

'You do know she's got a crush on you—don't you?'

'What?' Lincoln looked confused at the change in subject. 'Who?'

'Cassidy Yates, that's who.'

Lincoln shook his head in bewilderment. 'No, she doesn't—that's ridiculous.'

Amy banged her hand on the table. 'Oh, yes, she does! I can see it every time she looks at you.'

Lincoln slammed down his glass, sloshing root beer all over the table. 'And why does it matter? Why does it matter if she does have a crush on me? Why does it matter to you?'

She could feel her lips trembling and her hands begin to shake. He was angry. She'd never seen Lincoln angry before.

And it knocked the wind clean out of her sails.

He pushed himself up. 'This isn't about Cassidy Yates. This could *never* be about Cassidy Yates. This is about you and me, Amy. Don't pretend it's anything else.'

She could see the fire in his eyes, the pent-up frustration so tangible she could almost reach out and touch it.

Something gripped around her heart, squeezing it tightly. Could she tell him that she loved him? Could she say that right now she couldn't bear to be in the same room as him because she ached for his touch? Could she tell him that she wished she could turn back the clock six years?

No. No, she couldn't. Because Lincoln didn't need half a woman. He needed a whole one. He didn't need a woman who was carrying someone else's baby—a woman who would never be able to have any more natural children. He needed someone else, he *deserved* someone else. Someone who could give him children of his own.

But being around him and knowing that hurt like hell.

She had to get of there.

'I can't do this, Linc.' She stood up and slid out from the booth. 'I can't do this right now.' Her shaky voice grew firm, determined. 'This isn't a good time.' Her hands rested on her belly. 'I need to concentrate on this. I need to concentrate on *him*. Nothing is more important than this baby. I can't let anything else confuse me.' Try as she may and no matter how steady her voice was, she couldn't meet his gaze. One look into those eyes right now and she could crumble.

Lincoln's voice was barely contained. 'So I "confuse" you now? That's rubbish and you know it.' He came around and stood directly in front of her, his hands touching her shoulders. 'Tell me, Amy. Tell me how you feel.'

Her resolve started to shatter underneath her. Tears started to spill down her cheeks again. 'I don't know. I don't know how I feel. I don't know if any of these feelings are real, or if they're just a huge rush of hormones and nostalgia.' She flung her arms out in frustration, then raised her hands to her temples. She winced as her fingers touched the sides of her forehead. 'I can't sort anything out in my head right now. I can't think. I can't concentrate.' She shook her head furiously. 'I can't get rid of this damn headache!'

Her eyes finally met his. 'I didn't come here for me, Lincoln. I didn't come here for you. I came here...' she pressed her hands to her belly again '...for my son.'

Lincoln threw his hands up in frustration. He couldn't stand this any longer. He'd spent the last few days tiptoeing around her. Keeping his distance—even though it was killing him. Giving her space, giving her time.

'So this is all about the baby? Nothing else?'

'I can't let it be.'

The heavy silence pressed in on them as they stared at each other in the dimly lit room.

Lincoln wanted to storm out. He didn't need this. Six years of wishing you could see someone again, talk to them. And this was it.

Someone who pretended things weren't happening. Someone who tried to put a cap on their emotions. Someone who wouldn't face up to the facts between them. Someone who wouldn't even give him a chance. Enough was enough.

The headache was pounding in her ears. The breath in her chest started to tighten. Zachary started kicking, as if he could feel it too. Her head was swimming and heat started to creep over her body. What was this?

Blackness crept into the edges of her eyes. She blinked twice. Had some lights just gone out? Then panic crept across her chest. Her legs starting to buckle underneath her. 'Lincoln...'

He looked upwards just as she crumpled to a heap on the floor—too late to save her from smacking her head on the thick wooden planks. *'Johnny!'*

He turned her on her left hand side, making sure her airway was clear and checking her pulse. *'Get me an ambulance!'* His hands fell to her abdomen, feeling the little life inside pushing against him.

He squeezed his eyes tightly shut as guilt engulfed him. This could be a dozen different things, but he knew right now which one it would be—eclampsia. The headache, she'd said she had a headache and he hadn't listened. She'd been checked that morning at the hospital, but this was new, this was a different complaint and one that could be a sign of eclampsia. One that should have made him take her straight back to hospital.

Instead he'd been too self-absorbed. Too worried about developing a relationship with her that would meet his own needs. Too worried that she wouldn't tell him how she felt. He'd been angry. Shouted at her, probably raised her blood pressure.

He'd promised to look after her baby. He'd promised her a safe delivery.

Her body started to twitch. The first signs of a seizure. What had he done? Lincoln watched as things started to slip through his fingers—like the grains of sand on the beach.

He lifted his head. *'Where the hell is that ambulance?'*

CHAPTER EIGHT

LINCOLN shifted his position, his aching limbs objecting to the firm hard-backed chair. Was it possible his body was getting used to no sleep?

A little grunt came from under his chin. Baby Carson wriggled in the strip of cloth currently cocooning him against Lincoln's bare chest. It was almost as if the baby could hear the steadying beat of Lincoln's heart and was trying to get closer to it. He could feel the heat from his body wrap around the little figure, currently nestled under his shirt. He, better than anyone, knew that kangaroo care offered a huge range of benefits for pre-term babies—normalising temperature, heart and respiratory rate, decreasing stress, reducing risks of infection and promoting earlier discharge for premature babies. As a neonatologist he was a huge advocate for the technique. But he'd never actually done it himself. He'd never actually been the one sitting in the dead of night with a three-pound baby strapped to his chest. He swallowed the lump in his throat. He had to do this. He had to do this for Amy.

Cassidy Yates touched his shoulder. 'How you doing, Linc?' She sat down in the chair next to him, her blonde hair pulled backwards in a bun, her eyes lined and tired.

He moved forward to speak, but a little squeak from the baby made him shift back to his original position. 'Is something wrong?' His voice was strained. *Please let Amy be okay.*

Cassidy shook her head. 'There's no change, Linc. She still hasn't woken up.' Cassidy gave a sigh. 'It's only been forty-eight hours.' A tight smile appeared on her face. 'She'll wake up today. I know she will.'

The words hung in the air between them. Both of them hoping they'd be true.

Lincoln brushed his hand against hers. 'This is my fault, Cassidy, not yours. I was the one who took her out to dinner. I was the one she got into a fight with. I didn't even realise she had any other symptoms.' He moved his hand back and ran it through his hair. 'If I'd been paying enough attention…'

'Stop it, Linc. I was her obstetrician. I should have admitted her.'

Lincoln shook his head. 'But why? You'd monitored her every day. There had been no change in her symptoms. What reason could you have for admitting her?'

Cassidy sighed. 'Good old-fashioned instinct. I knew this wasn't going to turn out well. I let Amy down.'

Lincoln looked at the little bundle under his chin. He reached up and stroked a gentle finger across the top of the baby's soft fontanel. The first few sprigs of dark hair were just starting to appear.

Cassidy leaned forward in her chair, staring at Linc with her weary eyes. 'I told her to phone me as soon as any other symptoms appeared. How long did she have that headache, Linc? Why didn't she phone me?'

Because of me. Guilt tightened across his chest. Cassidy hadn't slept in the last two days. She was worried sick. She felt guilty—as if she'd made a mistake. But she hadn't. *He had.*

Deep down he knew why Amy hadn't phoned. She

hadn't been focusing on her symptoms. She'd been fixated on the fact that she thought something was happening
between Lincoln and Cassidy. *She'd been jealous.* And it
had affected her relationship with her obstetrician.

Lincoln cringed. He couldn't believe it had come to this.

Seeing Amy lying on the floor of the restaurant, seizing, had been the single most terrifying moment of his
life. Never had a five-minute ambulance journey seemed
so long.

And the E.R. events that had followed had felt like an
out-of-body experience. For once, he hadn't been in control. He'd watched as they'd put her on monitors, inserted
IVs and catheters, and stabilised her. Once the seizure had
been under control, a quick confab with Cassidy and the
anaesthetist had resulted in a rapid trip to Theatre and an
emergency Caesarean section.

Two hours after he'd brought her in her son had been
screaming in his gloved hands in the operating room.

And then he'd made the biggest decision of his life.
Because that's when it hit him. Like a lightning bolt. He
loved her.

And he couldn't be the baby's doctor. No matter what
he'd promised Amy, he couldn't be the neonatologist her
child needed.

He'd too much emotional investment in this. And it
would ruin his objectivity.

Yes, he could stand on the sidelines and discuss clinical decisions with the surrounding physicians but he had
to step back. He had to take himself out of the equation.
Because he didn't feel like a doctor around Amy's son. He
felt like a parent.

But the one thing Amy had asked him to do was be
her son's doctor. And chances were she would never forgive him.

Cassidy stood up again. 'I'm going back to ICU. She's going to wake up today. I want to be there.' Her voice was steady and determined, but Lincoln didn't know if she was trying to convince him or herself.

His hands cradled the little baby next to his chest. In most cases kangaroo care was carried out by the mother. But in this case, while Amy was unavailable, it seemed the most natural thing for him to be doing.

But he'd had no idea it would feel like this. The feel of the tiny translucent skin against his, the feeling of the little body warming against his, had swamped him. All this time he'd only really thought about Amy. He hadn't really brought her son into the equation. And now he was here, front and centre, and for the first time in his life Lincoln hadn't been able to distance himself into professional mode. He hadn't been able to sit on the sidelines and watch. He'd had to make sure he was in the middle of it all. No one else was allowed to carry out care for the baby.

And it would be easy right now to pretend this was all about guilt, and that he felt he owed it to Amy to look after her little boy. If that was how he felt, he could have stayed in doctor mode, in clinical mode, and done the best job that he could. But it wasn't how he felt. He could see Amy in this baby. And all the feelings he felt for her, whether he'd vocalised them or not, seemed to be intensified into this tiny body. Who could have known it could feel like this?

He'd often heard parents talk about being swamped by their feelings. But he'd never experienced it. Not like this. And he couldn't even begin to explain it. He had no genetic connection to this child. He had no parental rights. Amy could wake up today and tell him she never wanted to see him again. And he knew all of that. But it didn't change how he felt.

He shifted the little feeding tube currently taped to the side of the baby's nose. Amy had wanted to breastfeed her baby, so they'd used some of the breast milk available in the NICU, but so far Junior hadn't responded to cup feeding or finger feeding and with a premature baby time was of the essence, so they'd had to resort to placing a small tube down into his stomach. So every few hours Lincoln got a small syringe and fed Amy's son tiny amounts of breast milk. Anything to help him.

'Okay, Junior, let's get you back inside your incubator for a while. I need to go and see your mommy.'

He glanced down at his rumpled clothes—the same shirt and jeans he'd been wearing when Amy had seized in the restaurant two days ago. He really needed to get changed.

Lincoln placed the baby carefully back inside the incubator, pulling a little blue hat over his head. He checked the chart hanging at the end of the crib. Baby Carson was actually doing quite well. His weight at three pounds eight ounces was good, and gave him a ninety-five per cent survival rate. The steroids had obviously done their job of maturing his lungs and he'd come out screaming and breathing on his own. There had only been a few incidences when he'd tried to feed that his oxygen saturation had dropped. And since he'd had the tube put down, there had been none.

The little guy had fighting spirit. Now, if only he had a name.

But Amy hadn't told him what she was going to name her son—she'd expected to be there to do that herself.

Lincoln felt the small hand wrap itself around his finger. *Please let her wake up soon.*

Amy felt weird. She was having a dream. But instead of a nice, pink, floaty dream, this was a strange, distant far-away dream. And her throat ached. Her mouth was dry and felt brittle and she couldn't even swallow. Her head was pounding and noises were disturbing her peaceful sleep. She couldn't concentrate. Maybe if she could just have a drink of water...

Her eyes felt heavy, crusted, and she struggled to pull her eyelids apart. White. That was all she could see. *What was that?*

She moved her hands. Something was hurting her wrist. Like a little pinch, a little squeeze. Her hands moved to her stomach, seeking the comfort of the rounded bump she'd spent the last few months embracing. The firmness was gone. In its place only soft sagging skin. Alarm bells started racing in her head. Something wasn't right. Where was she? What was happening?

She could feel something pressing on her face and she reached up to pull it aside. She started struggling to breathe, taking short, rapid breaths. A figure appeared in her line of vision. Blonde. Boobs. Was it Barbie?

The voice was talking, but she wasn't sure what it was saying. A strong, calm voice. 'Amy. Amy. Calm down. Everything's fine. It's Cassidy Yates. You're in hospital— in San Francisco Maternity. Here...let me put this mask back on your face for a few moments.' The figure moved around to the side. 'I'm going to raise your bed slightly, Amy.' There was a buzzing noise and Amy felt herself move upwards. The white view changed to a hospital scene.

A hospital scene she should be familiar with. A busy ICU. As a former theatre nurse she'd spent many hours transferring patients to and from Theatre to ICU and back again. But even the familiarity didn't help.

There was a sense that something was wrong. She didn't feel right. She felt...empty.

Then it struck her. Her brain shifted sharply into focus and a million panicked thoughts filling her mind. 'My baby? Where's my baby?' Although she felt as if she was shouting, her voice was quiet, barely a whisper.

Cassidy leaned forward, touching her hand and squeezing it tightly. 'Your son is fine, Amy. He's in NICU. Lincoln's with him—I don't think he's left his side in the last forty-eight hours.'

Amy blinked. This wasn't real. This couldn't be happening. What did she mean—the last forty-eight hours?

The confusion must have registered on her face. Cassidy kept hold of her hand. 'Amy, do you remember anything about what happened?'

Amy shook her head. Her mind was currently mush. She couldn't take in where she was, let alone anything else.

Cassidy bent closer, reaching up and moving some loose strands of hair from her face. Why was this woman being so nice to her? Something turned inside her stomach. *She didn't like this woman*, but she couldn't remember why.

Her eyes went downwards. There was an IV in her hand. That's what the strange feeling was at her wrist. The tape surrounding it was catching the little hairs on her wrist. Tiny pieces of the jigsaw puzzle started slotting into place in her brain. Cassidy was talking again. 'You had a seizure, Amy. Two days ago. Lincoln brought you in, we stabilised you, then we had to take you to Theatre and deliver your baby. You've been in here ever since.'

Amy clung to the one part that registered in her brain. 'Zachary. How is Zachary?'

Cassidy's face broke into a smile. 'Zachary? That's what you're calling your son? What a beautiful name.' She glanced over her shoulder. 'Lincoln will be so pleased to hear it. He's been calling him Junior these last two days.'

Amy tried to pull her dry lips together again. 'Lincoln's looking after my son?'

Something registered on Cassidy's face. A fleeting glance, as if she shouldn't say something. But she pressed her lips together. 'Yes…and no.' It took her a few seconds to decide what to say. 'He's not your son's doctor. But he's been acting as a…surrogate parent for the last two days. He hasn't left Zachary's side. He's been doing all the kangaroo care for your son.'

Images flooded into Amy's mind. Her brain was still befuddled. Lincoln with her baby. Holding her baby, feeding her baby. She knew Zach would have been in safe hands. But hadn't he promised to be her baby's doctor?

'I don't understand…'

Cassidy stood upright, the relief on her face obvious. 'Oh, good, he's here. I'll let him speak to you himself.' She gave a final squeeze to Amy's hand. 'I'll come back later—to talk with you about your treatment.'

She walked towards Lincoln and gave his shoulder a little squeeze on the way past.

Amy watched as the green-suited figure appeared in the doorway. Her eyes were taking a little time to focus. Why was that?

Then she felt him engulf her in a hug, pulling her head and shoulders clear of the bed and into his chest. He held her so tightly she started to cough.

He released her quickly. 'Sorry. I'm just so pleased you've woken up. I've been so worried.' He clasped her hands, words tumbling from his mouth. 'The baby's doing well. He's breathing on his own—right from delivery—and he's a good weight for twenty-nine weeks: three pounds eight ounces. He's not feeding on his own yet, we've had to put a tube down, but I've made sure that he's getting breast milk. Oh, and you need to tell me his name, so I can put it in his records.'

Lincoln. It was definitely Lincoln. He was babbling. She didn't have any problem focusing up close. She could see his green theatre scrubs, his tousled dark hair and blue-rimmed, tired eyes. There was a definite shadow around his jaw—she'd felt it brush her cheek as he'd hugged her.

She blinked, focusing further—giving her brain time to make sense of it all in her head. She could see the deep lines etched into his forehead and filtering out from the corners of his eyes. Had they always been there? He looked exhausted.

She blinked. And in that instant there was something else. A fleeting picture of a darkened restaurant and a smell...a strong smell of fresh fish. The memory gave her a jolt, startling other little pieces of the jigsaw puzzle into place. An expression on Lincoln's face that she didn't recognise. He'd been angry with her. They'd been fighting.

That's why he looked like hell.

His fingers touched the inside of her palm. 'Amy, are you with me?' The anxiety was back.

She nodded, her dry tongue coming out and trying to lick her lips. He responded instantly, picking up a glass of iced water with a straw from her bedside table. Where had that come from?

He held the straw at her lips and she sucked deeply. 'Steady,' he said, pulling it away for a second then bringing it back to her again. He let her take some more sips. 'Better?'

She nodded and let out a sigh. 'Zachary. Zachary John Carson. That's my son's name.'

His eyes met hers and he nodded in recognition. 'It's a beautiful name.'

'I want to see him.' Now she'd found her voice again, it was steely and determined. A wave of emotions rode up inside her, like a crest of a wave. She'd missed the first two days of her son's life. She hadn't been the first person to hold him, to hear him cry or feed him. She'd missed so much already. 'I want to see him now.'

Lincoln hesitated. 'You've just woken up, Amy, I don't think you're stable enough to go to NICU. And I'm sorry, but I can't bring Zachary in here.' He waved his hand around the ICU. There were four other adult patients in the room. One was attached to a ventilator—that must have been the burring noise that she'd heard—and two others had assisted ventilation. 'There's too big a risk of exposure to infection.'

Amy knew he was being eminently sensible. But forty-eight hours' worth of post-birth hormones didn't care. 'I *need* to see my son.'

Something washed over Lincoln's face. Guilt. Why did he feel guilty? 'I know you do, Amy.' His hand was still pressed next to hers. 'Let me see what I can arrange. I promise you'll see your son soon.'

For a second she thought he was going to bend over and kiss her. But he hesitated midway across the bed, pulling back and heading out the door in his green scrubs.

And that's when the floodgates opened.

Two hours later she was ensconced in a side room. Lincoln pushed the neonate crib into the room and Amy's breath caught in her throat. Her son.

That tiny little scrap she could see through the plastic was hers. Her baby. Wrapped in a pale blue blanket with a tiny knitted cap on his head. Fists punching angrily in the air. And a tiny plastic tube coming from his nose and taped to the side of his cheek.

Her breast ached. She wanted to feed her baby. She wanted to feel his little body next to hers. She could feel her lips tremble as Lincoln lifted him out of the crib and handed him to her.

Zachary gave a little groan and snuggled towards her—a natural response. She felt transfixed. His little eyes were screwed up, his skin pale just like hers, a few tiny strands of dark hair on his head. The wrinkled forehead smoothed out and his eyes blinked open, staring upright straight into her eyes. Her heart gave a little flutter at the blue eyes, then she realised that all babies were born with blue eyes. His eye colour could change over the next year. The thought brought a little smile to her face.

The next year. She was going to spend all that time with her son. She might have missed the first few days but there was nothing to stop her now. A little warmth spread across her chest. She lifted her finger and stroked it down her son's button nose. He was all hers. Six years she'd waited for this moment, and now she finally had her child in her arms.

Lincoln shifted his feet beside her, obviously not wanting to interrupt her first few moments with her son. She blinked back the tears forming in her eyes. 'Thank you for looking after him,' she whispered.

He looked uncomfortable. He sat down in the chair next to her bed, bringing him level with her. 'I need to tell you something.'

'What?' She couldn't take her eyes from her son.

'I couldn't do what you wanted me to.'

Cassidy's words started to float around her brain again. This time, though, they started to register. Something about Lincoln not being her baby's doctor…

She found the little hospital band attached to his tiny wrist and rotated it. Baby Carson. Three pounds eight ounces. And his date of birth. Dr Lomax. Who was Dr Lomax?

A surge of anger struck her. Her cold stare fixed on Lincoln. 'What is it you want to tell me, Lincoln?'

She could see the pain on his face. This wasn't easy for him—but right now she didn't care. She'd asked him to do one thing for her. One thing. She'd travelled miles to find him, to find the best doctor to look after her son—and now this.

He ran his fingers through his hair the way he always did when he was nervous. 'I'm really sorry, Amy. This is all my fault. I should have kept a better eye on you—I shouldn't have taken you out to dinner. This would never have happened if I'd kept in the role I should have—as the doctor for your son.' He shook his head and lifted his eyes to meet hers. 'But I just couldn't.'

Amy took a breath. The air felt tight in her chest. 'What do you mean, this is all your fault? How is any of this your fault? Lincoln, you let me stay in your apartment—you drove me to hospital every day, how can you possibly think this is your fault?'

'Your headache. You told me you had a headache and I ignored the signs, something a doctor on his game would never have done. I could have got you to hospital sooner. I should have been paying attention.'

She shook her head. '*I* should have paid more attention. Not you. I'd had that headache all day, but I thought it was nothing. Cassidy warned me—she gave me a list of signs and symptoms to look out for, and told me to come straight back to hospital if I developed any of them. But it seemed so mild, so subtle. It didn't even start to bother me until later in the day. I honestly thought it was just a headache. I never thought it would lead to this.' She glanced down at the bundle in her arms. 'Do you honestly think I would have put my son at risk? The headache was so mild that I hadn't even thought about taking anything until we were out. Up until then it really felt like nothing.'

The lines in his forehead were deeper than normal. She was doing nothing to alleviate his guilt. What else did he want to tell her?

Lincoln leaned forward in the chair, resting his arms on the side of her bed. 'When I saw you seizing…it was the worst five minutes of my life. By the time we got here and stabilised you then made the decision to take you to Theatre, I knew I couldn't be Zach's doctor.'

'What do you mean, you couldn't be my son's doctor?' Her voice had a cold, hard edge to it. 'It was the one thing I asked you to do for me, Lincoln. It was the *only* thing I asked you to do for me.'

'I know, I know.' The anguish in his voice was apparent, and she knew he was struggling to find the words.

'Who is Dr Lomax, Lincoln?'

'He's my colleague. My friend—someone I would trust with my child's life. As soon as I held Zach in my arms in Theatre, I knew I had to get someone else to do the job. I couldn't think straight. I couldn't think like a doctor while I was looking at him. I couldn't be the professional that I needed to be. I couldn't step back and see the wider picture. All I could see was the woman I loved lying on the operating table and her twenty-nine-week-old son in my hands. I knew I had to get someone else to do the job.'

His words hung in the air.

He loved her. He'd said it. Words that she'd been waiting to hear. So why wasn't she jumping for joy? Why wasn't she shouting it from the rooftops?

He was looking at her, waiting for her to respond. She tried to sort out her brain. She wanted to tell him that she loved him too. But something was stopping her. Something was pressing down on her chest, willing her not to say those words.

She kept her eyes on her baby. She didn't want to look at those dark-rimmed blue eyes. She didn't want them to pull her in and say something she would later regret.

Her son was staring up at her. Could he see her yet? Could he see the anguish on her face? How well could a twenty-nine-weeker see?

'Cassidy said that you'd looked after him, that you'd done kangaroo care. That you hadn't left his side for forty-eight hours.'

'I couldn't be his doctor, Amy, but that doesn't mean I don't care—it means I care too much. I didn't want anyone else to do his care. I wanted to be by his side. I wanted to watch over him. I wanted to feed him.'

A single tear slid down her face. It was just as she'd feared. He was professing not only his love for her but for Zach too. This should be what happy endings were about. But she still couldn't lift her head to meet his gaze.

Her feelings for him were so strong. Since the first time she'd seen him again, all her thoughts and memories of him had increased tenfold. He was everything she could ever want.

But what did that make her to him?

She didn't want to be his charity case. His poor ex with a baby he felt sorry for. He was feeling guilty right now. Guilt that he was confusing with love. He didn't love her. She wasn't the whole, healthy woman she'd been before.

She was damaged goods. Her body would never be the same again, even if she had the reconstruction surgery.

And Zach was it for her. She would never be able to have more natural kids. Her eggs were gone. Finished. And Lincoln…he was just starting out. He should have a whole brood of children of his own. And a happy, healthy wife who could give them to him.

She didn't want him to settle. She didn't want him to settle for her and Zachary. Even though it could make her happier than she'd thought possible, she wanted him to have the chance at life that she'd missed out on.

He stood up and moved to the side of the bed, sliding his arm around her shoulders and bending over to look down at Zach. 'Do you feel well enough to try the kangaroo care for a little while? Do you think you could manage him strapped next to your chest?'

She nodded. She couldn't speak right now. Words were just too difficult. He'd just stood up, not waiting for a response from her. He seemed to accept that she couldn't say the 'I love you' words back. What did that mean?

'Do you need some analgesia for your section wound before we start?'

She shook her head. The Caesarean section wound wasn't nearly as painful as she'd imagined. Maybe being unconscious for the first forty-eight hours had helped. The nurse had given her a couple of painkillers when she'd woken up and she felt fine.

Lincoln rummaged around in her locker. 'Let's find you something else to wear. That hospital gown won't do.'

He was right. The traditional hospital gown, with its Velcro fastenings at the back, wouldn't suit. He pulled out a pair of loose yellow jersey pyjamas, with buttons down the front. 'What about these?'

Amy nodded her head. Her tiny son was still in her arms. A nurse came into the room and between her and Lincoln they helped Amy freshen up and then secure her son next to her.

The next few hours passed swiftly. Amy tried to get

her tiny son to latch onto her breast, and when that failed, she managed to express some of her milk to feed to him via the tiny tube down his nose. The nurse rechecked her vital signs and reduced some of her IV infusions.

Cassidy came and checked on her twice. She talked her through the events and her subsequent care, warning her that women could still have seizures after delivery and that she would need to be observed for the next few days.

And Lincoln floated in and out of her room all day, taking Zachary back to the nursery for a spell then bringing him back to her later.

It was almost as if the words hadn't been spoken—or never been heard. Life was beginning to tick along as normal. Why did that make her feel so empty inside?

Lincoln wheeled the cot back along the corridor to NICU. Zachary was doing well and seemed a little brighter since his mother had woken up. Although he hadn't managed to latch on today, there was every chance that he'd start breastfeeding soon and then his tube could be removed.

So why did life feel at a standstill?

For Lincoln, the instant feeling of relief when Amy had woken up had now been replaced by a feeling of worthlessness. She didn't blame him for her deterioration, she hadn't even been too angry when he'd told her he couldn't be Zachary's doctor. In fact, she'd hardly said *anything*, even after his heart had been in his throat and he'd said those words. The *I love you* words.

And there had been nothing—no response. It was almost as if he hadn't spoken.

Lincoln looked at the little baby lying in the crib beneath him. Zachary Carson. Every day he grew more attached. Every day he noticed something else about the little guy. Something new.

But what if this was a recipe for disaster? Amy had never said anything to make him think she was looking for anything else from him.

He still couldn't get to the bottom of what Amy wanted and it frustrated him beyond belief. She'd come here saying she wanted his skills and expertise as a doctor. But from the moment they'd set eyes on each other again, the tension in the air had been palpable.

He loved it that she was unpredictable. He loved it that she flirted with him. He loved it that they still seemed to fit together like pieces in a jigsaw puzzle.

But Amy was different too. Illness had changed her. A high-risk pregnancy had changed her. She wasn't as confident as she used to be. Sure, he knew that her body had changed, but something else had changed deep inside her. Was it her feelings of self-worth? He just couldn't put his finger on it. He couldn't really understand. And it was making him tiptoe around about her, something he'd never had to do before.

Then there was the guilt. Guilt that she'd come to him for help and he'd let her down. He'd let his guard down. He didn't want to be Amy's son's doctor.

One of the NICU nurses walked past and gave him a little smile. Carrie. Blonde. Cute. Nice butt. The old Lincoln would have chased her out the door. The old Lincoln would have had her number in his phone in two minutes flat.

Lincoln moved into autopilot. He lifted Zachary from the crib, strapped him to his chest and nestled him under his shirt.

He had absolutely no doubt about where he wanted to be. The effect of seeing Amy again after six years had been like a punch to the face. No woman had made him feel the way she did. He hadn't recognised love because he'd never felt it before. He didn't know what to say to her, when to back off, or when to move closer.

This was a steep learning curve.

But he'd never been one to shirk a challenge—and this was one thing he was determined to master.

CHAPTER NINE

AMY swallowed nervously as she climbed the steps towards the apartment. Her arms couldn't hide the slight tremor in them as she carried her precious bundle upstairs to the place she was currently calling 'home'.

This was nothing like she'd imagined. Zachary was six weeks old—he shouldn't even have been born yet. But his feeding and weight gain had been sufficient for him to be discharged from San Francisco's Children's Hospital. His skin had lost that translucent look and his little body had finally managed to store a tiny amount of fat and fill out a little.

His wide blue eyes had obviously started to focus and she could see him studying her face at times and reacting to her expressions. And at five pounds he was even big enough to wear some of the premature baby clothes she'd carefully folded in a drawer in Lincoln's apartment.

But all of this still unsettled her. She was in San Francisco—this wasn't home to her—but it could be. The longer she stayed here, the more she loved this city, from its quirky visitors and attractions to its deep-rooted history and traditions. She loved looking over to the Golden Gate Bridge, she loved the bustling people around Pier 39. She loved the rattle of the cable cars. And most of all she loved the staff attached to San Francisco's Children and

Maternity Hospital. Unlike most hospitals, she'd yet to meet a member of staff who hadn't been warm and friendly, who hadn't made her feel at home. She was sure that being a good friend of one the consultants helped. But it was also a place she could see a future in, a place where she would be happy to go to work. So why the strange feeling in her stomach?

Lincoln had arranged for Zachary's baby items to be delivered to San Francisco from Santa Maria. Literally overnight the white wooden baby crib and chest of drawers had appeared in her bedroom in Lincoln's apartment. The zebra-print baby seat was currently sitting next to the sofa in the living room. And the red pram was parked at the bottom of the stairs. All awaiting the arrival of baby Zachary.

She thought that she would have loved this moment. To finally bring her son home from hospital was a huge step. She should be singing from the rooftops. She should be telling the whole world that Zach was well enough to come home. But she wasn't. She couldn't.

She was nervous. She felt sick. Her stomach was churning. Was this new-mother nerves? Or something else?

The patient, easily accessible staff in the NICU were no longer by her side. The emergency monitors and equipment were no longer ready to be pulled over at a moment's notice. All the little queries or insecurities she'd had in the last few weeks couldn't be answered by another person in the room. Or could they?

Because Lincoln was here with her. Lincoln hadn't left her side. Or Zachary's.

He'd done everything he could to help her. He'd bent over backwards to be accommodating. And as much as she was grateful, it was going to make it so much harder to say goodbye…

Because right now she knew that was what she had to do.

Lincoln slid his key into the lock in the door and pushed the buttons to turn off the alarm. He held the door wide for her. She gave a little smile and carried Zachary into the apartment, walking over to one of the huge windows. 'What do you think, Zach? Do you like this place?'

Because she certainly did. So why did she feel as if she had to leave? Why, when the man of her dreams was offering her love, did she feel as if she had to retreat to the distant hills? Why did she feel that she couldn't even enter into a discussion with him?

She carried Zach through to the bedroom. 'Here's your crib, right next to Mommy's bed. I'll be able to stick my hand through and hold your hand.' She held him up to look, but Zach just blinked.

Her attention was caught by something new. 'Wow, look at this.' She leaned over and touched the mobile hanging above the crib and turned on the music. The soft, multicoloured animals started to spin around to 'Nelly the Elephant'. 'Did you get this?' she asked Lincoln.

He nodded slowly, folding his arms and leaning against the doorpost. 'Colour and noise are supposed to stimulate babies.' That smile again. That smile that drew you in and held you there. Held you with those dark blue eyes.

Being around him was good. His easy way and infectious laugh made her feel comfortable. She'd fallen asleep in his arms several times over the last few weeks, resting in the chairs next to Zachary's crib in NICU, and woken to find her head on his chest and her arms wrapped around him.

The electricity between them was still there. He just wasn't acting on it.

And for some strange reason it hurt.

She knew it was all her fault. She hadn't reacted when he'd told her that he loved her. She'd stayed silent, and he must have been hurt by that. But what could she do? What could she offer him? A woman with an altered body? Someone who hadn't yet reached the golden 'five years cancer-free'? The chance to have no natural children of his own? Lincoln was a gorgeous, handsome man. He deserved to have a better future than the one she could offer him.

She already knew that he was becoming more attached to her and Zachary. If the last few weeks hadn't been so hard she might have got her act together and done something about it.

But she hadn't. And now here she was, in his apartment, with her baby son.

She felt an arm at her waist, but it was a casual movement, not an intimate one. Zachary's eyes were starting to close, so she pulled off his padded jacket and laid him down in his crib for the first time, leaning back against Lincoln to watch his eyelids finally flicker shut and his little body relax.

'It's been a big day.' His voice was warm, comforting, like a big blanket enveloping her.

'It has.' She sighed as she pressed the little night-light next to the crib. His first night home from hospital. Should she really be feeling so terrified?

'Want me to make dinner?'

All of sudden she felt exhausted. She wanted to lie down in the bed next to her son and watch him sleep. She wanted to watch his little chest rise and fall. She wanted to stretch her hand through the bars and let his little fingers wrap around her big one so they could hold each other while they slept. She shook her head. 'I'm not hungry, Linc. I just want to lie down.'

He gave her waist a little squeeze. 'You've got to keep your strength up. I have it on good authority that babies are hard work. How about I make you something light like scrambled eggs?' His hand lifted up and stroked the back of her neck in a soothing motion. 'It will take five minutes then you could soak in the bath if you wanted.'

A bath. A deep-filled bath overflowing with lavender scents and bubbles. That would be sheer bliss. She hadn't had a bath since she'd had Zachary. She always seemed to be racing in and out of the shower. It had seemed quicker, more convenient. This could be perfect.

She gave a little nod. 'Scrambled eggs would be good.' She stepped over towards the en suite bathroom and picked up the bottle of dark purple bubble bath, opening it, tipping a generous portion into the white roll-topped bath then turning the tap on full blast.

Ten minutes later, tummy full of scrambled eggs and a baby soundly sleeping, Amy stepped into the water and slid her body beneath the bubbles.

She would have a think about things tomorrow—sort everything out in her mind. Everything would seem clearer then and she would think about what to say to Lincoln. She could make plans about returning to Santa Maria and finding a paediatrician for her son. She would eventually have to think about childcare for Zachary—who would want to look after a baby that had been born premature? She would need childcare that could be flexible around her shifts. Would she be able to find anyone to do that? Maybe she should find a different job? Even the thoughts exhausted her. Tonight she just wanted to relax.

'Amy!'

The sharp knock on the door woke her with a jolt. Her brain took a few seconds to focus, obviously a few seconds too long because the door opened and Lincoln stuck his head through the gap. 'Is everything okay?'

Amy had sat bolt upright with the knock on the door, leaving her breast above the bubbled waterline and her flat side exposed. Her hands flew to her chest and she ducked beneath the bubbles again. 'Lincoln! Don't come in, I'm still in the bath!' Her cheeks flamed red. She must have dozed off as the water was now lukewarm. She leaned forward to grab a fluffy towel from beside the bath.

He must have seen her scar. He must have seen the empty side.

Lincoln pulled back. The panic on Amy's face was evident. He hadn't meant to embarrass her, he'd just wanted to check she was okay. Then he stopped. Took a deep breath, stepped into the bathroom and closed the door behind him.

'Lincoln! What are you doing?'

'Something I should have done weeks ago.'

He bent forward and picked up the towel she was grappling for, holding it open in front of him. 'Come on.'

Her flaming cheeks burned even harder. 'You've got to be joking.'

'No. I'm not.' His voice was firm and determined. He gestured with the towel once more. 'Come on, Amy.'

'No.' Her voice was sharp and to the point.

He stared at her.

'Don't, Lincoln. You're making me uncomfortable.'

He knelt down next to the bath so his face was level with hers. 'I'm not trying to make you uncomfortable, Amy. But this is an issue between us—you know it is. I'm not here to upset you. I'm your friend. I'm here to support you. Now, get out the bath so we can talk about this. Take the first step.' He held the towel out again.

Her bottom lip trembled. She didn't feel ready for this. She wanted to pull her knees up to her chest, tuck her chin on top and hide her body from the world. Why couldn't he be plain? Why couldn't he be ugly? Would that make it easier? Would it be easier to bare your blemished body to someone who didn't reek of perfection?

She bit her lip, a sheen across her eyes. *Take the first step.* How did he know exactly what to say? She had to be brave. He was right. He was getting right to the heart of the matter. It was an issue. She just didn't know if she could handle this.

There was only one way to do this. She had to try. She owed it to herself to try. She closed her eyes and stood upright, stepping out the bath almost simultaneously and moving across into the comfort of the white fluffy towel. He wrapped it around her and she caught the edges of it, pulling it closer and tucking it around her before she opened her eyes.

He gestured to the side of the bath. 'Sit down.' He picked up another towel and dried her bare legs. Had he even had a chance to get a proper look at her scarred body? What had he thought?

His arm went around her shoulders, escorting her from the bathroom and into his bedroom. *His bedroom.* She hadn't set foot in this room the whole time she'd been staying here. She felt the breath catch in her throat as he guided her over towards his bed, then her heart plummeted as he stood her in front of the free-standing, full-length mirror next to his bed. He raised his hand and pulled the cream blind at the window, plunging the room into semi-darkness, with some of the early evening sun still filtering through the blind.

All of a sudden she didn't feel so exhausted. Maybe the nap in the bath had revived her, but she didn't think so. Her blood was racing around her body. Why did this feel so natural? Why wasn't she terrified?

She'd been planning to leave. She'd been thinking about telling Lincoln a million reasons why she and Zachary shouldn't stay there. So why did this feel as though it should happen?

'Now.' He guided her in front of the mirror, standing behind her with his hands at her waist. 'What do you see?'

'What do you mean?'

His voice radiated calm. A man totally in control, who knew exactly what he was doing. 'I want you to look in the mirror and tell me what you see.'

She turned to face him. 'I can't. I don't want to do this any more.'

There it was on her face again. Panic. Put her in a situation out of her control and she floundered. He ran his finger down her cheek, the most delicate of touches. 'Yes, yes, you can.' He gently spun her around again. 'I'll tell you what I see.' His hands crept back around her waist, his tall body right behind hers, his strength and muscles running down the length of her body, his chin resting on her shoulder, staring at their joint reflections.

He smiled into the mirror and touched her hair. 'I see a beautiful woman, with gorgeous red tresses and magical green eyes.' He ran his finger along the skin at her neck. 'I see pale skin and a tiny splash of freckles across her nose.' His chin swapped round to the other side of her body, as if he was appreciating her from all angles. 'And I like the pale skin—because it's different. Most women here could die a death from fake tan—or a death from a real tan. I like it that your skin is completely natural and untouched by the sun. You don't need a tan. Your pure beauty radiates from your skin.'

His words danced like a song over her. Rising and falling, causing her heart to flutter in her chest one moment and her clenched stomach to flip over the next.

She looked at the reflection in the mirror. The pale face stared back at her. The tired eyes, the washed-out face. Why couldn't she see what he did?

She leaned backwards a little, relaxing into his strength. In some ways she hated this, and in others she knew that the time was right and this was exactly what she needed. And Lincoln was right—it was easier doing this with a friend.

His hands reached in front of her body to where the towel was tucked in. She flinched. No! She could see the fear in her own face in the mirror, but she was intrigued by his reflection. His fingers were gently untucking the towel, loosening it and lifting the edges, dropping the white towel to the floor and leaving her naked body exposed in front of the mirror.

And his face didn't look shocked, didn't look disgusted and didn't look repulsed. In fact, he bent and kissed the skin at the bottom of her neck, wrapping one arm around her waist, keeping her close to him.

He lifted his head again, staring at her in the mirror. 'Don't be afraid,' he whispered, a comforting smile on his face. Her hands were trembling again, she couldn't help it—she'd never felt so exposed. And although the room was warm, goose-bumps appeared all over her pale flesh.

His hand came up on one side and cupped her full breast. There was nothing sexual in his touch. Her breast was working overtime feeding her son right now and even the slightest touch could make milk leak. On the other side his fingers traced a light line up from her hip bone to under her arm, pausing for only a second before running along the flat, pale, white line of her scar—where her breast should be.

Her eyes took in her reflection. Six weeks on from giving birth and her lower body had started to return to normal. Her stomach wasn't flat. It probably never would be again and there was a small, visible red scar running along her bikini line. But it was a neat scar, well healed and already starting to retreat into her body. In a few years' time it would be pale and virtually unnoticeable. Unlike the scar at her breast. A visible marker of something missing.

He kissed her neck again whilst his fingers danced along her skin. And he kept on kissing her as his hands gently caressed her. She was caught, watching the reflection in the mirror of a handsome man touching a lover's body. There was no shame. No horror. Like a slow movie scene, with romantic music playing. Only this time, instead of music, it was one word repeating itself over and over in her head. *Acceptance.*

The kisses reached the bottom of her throat. The hand left her full breast—as if he knew it was too sensitive for touch right now—and reached up to tangle in her red curls. He moved, lifting up her arm on her affected side and looping it around behind his neck. Then he watched in the mirror as he ran his fingers once more down her side. Another woman might have flinched at the light, tickling sensations. But for Amy it was different. It was all about acceptance. And it wasn't about his acceptance of her. It was about her acceptance of her changed body.

She was staring at the reflection in front of her. And the old sensations were gone. And she didn't see something to be ashamed of. She didn't see something she should hide from the world. This wasn't something she would ever share. But it was something that she didn't need to hide away from any more. For the first time in six years she could look at her naked body without feeling fear or repulsion. This was a woman who had the right to be loved.

Her hand moved from behind his neck to run through his hair. The movement caused her to lean backwards, exposing even more of the sensitive flesh at the base of her neck to his lips. She wasn't looking in the mirror any more. She was losing herself in the feelings.

'This is the body of the woman that I love. This is the body of a vibrant, healthy and whole woman.' His fingers went to her flat surface again. 'This is only a tiny part of Amy. And I don't care if you decide to have reconstruction surgery or not. I will take you however you come. If it matters to you then fine. But don't change anything for me, because I love you just the way you are.'

He spun her round, hands at her waist. He looked her straight in the eye. He moved forward, pressing himself against her. She was naked and he was still fully clothed. But she could feel his hard length through his jeans, pressing against her abdomen. A smile came across her lips.

He was hard. He was very hard. It didn't matter that she felt her body was disfigured. It didn't matter that she felt she had to hide. The proof was right in front of her—literally. She turned him on. He wanted her.

She felt twenty-five again. She felt young and whole. The way she used to feel when she'd danced around his cabin naked. Her fingers moved and unfastened the buttons on his jeans, releasing him into her hands.

For the first time in five years she felt powerful. She felt sexual. It was a glimmer of what she'd felt in that hospital room the last time they'd kissed. Control. She felt in control.

He was staring at her, with those sexy, half-shut eyes. Even if she'd been on the other side of the room, those eyes alone could have turned her on. But right now his fingers were moving lower. Going from one set of red curls to another. She moved closer. She wasn't going to flinch at his touch now. This was what she wanted. She was ready.

She'd had her six-week postnatal check. Everything was

as it should be. There was no reason she couldn't have sex. And from the way her body was currently responding, it was telling her it was time.

He reached his hands up to either side of her head. His eyes fixed on hers. 'Are you sure?' he whispered. 'We only do this if you want to—you're in charge.' There was a glimmer in his eye. He knew exactly what he was doing. He was giving her all the control—and it was sexy as hell.

She tilted her head to one side, her eyes glancing down at the prize possession in her hands. 'I want to see what I'm getting.' She whipped his T-shirt up and pulled it over his head, revealing his muscular torso. Her hands pressed against him. 'Not too shabby,' she whispered with a glint in her eye.

She pushed him backwards onto the bed, climbing above him. 'So *I'm* in charge?' she questioned.

His smile revealed his straight white teeth. 'Absolutely.'

'Good. Then this is what we're going to do...'

The early morning sunlight was filtering through the blind again. Amy had been up twice in the night to feed and change Zachary, and on each occasion he'd settled back down to sleep quickly.

It would have been nice to wake up in Lincoln's arms and feel his body heat next to hers, but the reality of a premature baby dictated how things would work out.

Last night had been cathartic for her. She'd finally got to the place she needed to. She'd felt desired, wanted, sexual. She'd felt loved. But the early morning light brought a whole new range of issues with it. Issues where she'd barely even scratched the surface. She threw back the white duvet and swung her legs out of the bed. Her feet padded across the dark wooden floor and she stopped in the doorway of Lincoln's room.

His long, lean naked body was entwined around his duvet cover. It looked like one of those ultra-trendy pictures you could buy in black and white and put on your wall. His chest was rising and falling and there was a dark shadow around his chin where the stubble was starting to appear. He was picture-perfect.

She moved in front of the free-standing mirror where he'd undressed her last night. She released the belt on the fluffy white dressing gown and let it fall open. She stared at her reflection. One round full breast and one flat white scar. Her finger traced along the line of the scar. Even now, after everything that had happened, it still made a little shiver go down her spine. Last night Lincoln had shown her acceptance. Acceptance for who she was now. She kept staring, her breathing and heart rate quickening. She didn't like the image in the mirror. She didn't like the person staring back at her. Lincoln may have shown her acceptance but in the cold light of day she couldn't accept herself. She couldn't accept the reflection in the mirror.

Last night may have been wonderful, but it was only the start of the journey for her.

She could hear his breathing behind her. It could be so easy if she could just push all this aside and forget about it. It would be so easy to climb into bed next to him and snuggle into his arms. But this was never going to go away.

What was wrong? Why did her life feel like sand running through her fingers on the beach? How could she explain that to him? How could she tell him that no matter how good he was to her and Zachary, right now she needed to be on her own. How could she tell him she had to leave?

This was killing her. She'd thought that the cancer might kill her and she'd beaten that. But this was causing her more pain than the cancer ever had. More pain than the surgery and more pain than the chemotherapy and radio-therapy put together. And the worst thing about this was that she was the only person who could feel it. She wanted to feel free, she wanted to feel easy with herself. More than anything she wanted to have a happy family life. And she knew without a shadow of a doubt that Lincoln loved Zachary as if he were his own.

That's what made this so hard.

She had to step away. She didn't want to hurt him, but if she stayed without facing her demons she couldn't predict their future.

She wanted to be with Lincoln because she loved him. Not because he was the easy way for her to deal with her past illness. It wasn't true to herself and it wasn't fair to him. If she tried to deal with how she felt while staying with Lincoln, it could cloud her judgement and influence her decisions. She needed to step away. And she needed to do it before he became even more attached to Zach.

What if he met someone else? Someone who could give him a family of his own? The thought made her stomach churn. It was a risk she had to take.

She wanted to love Lincoln with her whole heart, not just the little piece she hadn't locked away.

His eyelids flickered open and a lazy smile appeared across his face. He lifted the corner of the twisted duvet. 'Wanna come in?'

She shook her head, but walked over towards him and sat on the edge of the bed. 'Morning.' Her voice was cool.

He rested his head on his hand. 'What's up? Something wrong with Zachary?'

'No, he's fine.' She smoothed her hand along the bed, focusing on the crumpled sheet rather than his face. 'He's sleeping again.'

'So why don't you come back to bed?' There was a

twinkle in his eye again and it pulled at her heartstrings. She didn't want to hurt him. He'd helped her in more ways than he could ever imagine.

She took a deep breath and stood up, turning to face him. She had to be calm, she had to be in control. 'I have to leave, Lincoln.'

The words came like a bolt out of the blue, causing him to sit upright and swing his legs out of the bed. So much for a lazy morning. 'What on earth are you talking about?'

'I can't stay here any more. You've been so kind, but I need some time—some space.'

Deep lines of utter confusion furrowed Lincoln's brow. 'We go from last night—to this? Did I do something wrong?'

She shook her head and touched his arm. 'No, Linc. You didn't. You did something wonderful. But that's what's wrong. I've spent five years avoiding this. I've spent five years not dealing with this. And I can't move on. I can't move on to the next stage of my life without dealing with this first.'

'So why can't we deal with it together?'

She sighed. 'Because there can't be an "us". There can't be a "together". I've got to take some time to learn to accept who I am and what I've been through. And I've got to do it on my own. I've got to do this on my own terms.'

'Why on earth do you think you've got to do this yourself? I told you last night that I was happy to take you the way you are.'

She sat down next to him. 'I know you did, Lincoln.' She looked down at the space where her breast should be. 'You're happy to take me the way I am...' she looked at him with tear-glazed eyes '...but I'm not. This isn't about you. It's about me.'

'Don't give me the "it's not you, it's me" speech. You owe me better than that.'

She bit her lip. 'I know I do, Linc. And I'm sorry. Ultimately, I truly want us to be together. I want us to be family. But I've got to be selfish about this because right now I know I'm not ready and I've got to look after me first.'

'And you think this is the way? You think this is the answer? To go away? Hell, Amy, you're just out of hospital with a premature baby—do you really think this is the time to find yourself?' He was pacing around the room now in his white jersey shorts, agitated. She had to pull her eyes away.

But he hadn't finished. 'I've spent six weeks—*six weeks*—helping look after your son. And now you're just going to take him away from me?' His pacing grew more frenetic. 'I'm the one who's spent the most time with him, and I know I don't have any rights to him, I know Zachary isn't mine. But he feels like mine. He *feels* like my son. I can't just let you walk away. Zach knows me, he recognises me—how can this be good for him?'

Amy could feel a tear trickle from the corner of her eye. This was harder than she'd ever imagined. Her heart was breaking. She'd never wanted this for Linc. She'd never wanted to hurt him. But that was exactly what she was doing. She'd come to him because she'd thought he'd be the best doctor for her son. But things had changed so much. This hadn't really been about healing her son, this had been about healing herself.

'This is about Zachary, Linc. This is all about Zachary. How can I be a good mother to him when I can't even look at my reflection in the mirror? How can I focus my time and attention on my son when this is hanging in the background? How can I even think about another relationship when I'm still not comfortable in my own skin?

'I want to be free to love you. I want to be free to watch you have a relationship with my son. But everything inside me is so screwed up. I need to go back home—home to Santa Maria and my friends. I need to learn to look after myself and Zach before I'm ready to do this. Don't you see what you've done for me? The best thing in the world. You've helped me realise I need to face up to my demons. I'm healthy, Linc. Physically, I'm healthy. And I hope that when I reach my five-year anniversary I'll be able to kiss my breast cancer goodbye completely. But inside?' She shook her head.

'I'm not quite there yet.' She lifted a finger and touched the side of his cheek—gently, tenderly. 'I need to take one last step. This is the final hurdle. The last thing I need to overcome. And you've given me the courage to do it. I want to have a relationship with you. I do. But right now I'm short-changing you. I'm not loving you the way I should. You need to let me go. You need to let me go and come back on my own terms.'

He stopped pacing and stared at her. She couldn't read his face. It was as if he was trying to make sense of her words. As if he was trying to rationalise what she was saying—trying to construct an argument against it. She could see the tension across the muscles in his shoulders and his abdomen. He was upset.

Then she saw his shoulders sag, his muscles relax. It was as if he'd resigned himself to the fact she wanted to leave. As if he understood her words and realised this was the only way.

And it caused her tears to flow even stronger.

He reached over and brushed a loose curl from her cheek, tucking it behind her ear. She could see a million thoughts in his eyes. He leaned forward. 'Sometimes the hardest bridge to cross is the one in your own mind.' His words were quiet, almost a whisper. 'I can't do this for you.'

'I know.' The words hung in the air between them, like a moment of suspended time.

He brushed a kiss to her cheek. 'If this is what you need, then I can't pretend to understand, but I'll always support you. You and Zach.'

He lifted his head. 'When do you want to go?' He hesitated. 'I want to say goodbye to Zach.'

She breathed a huge sigh of relief. It almost felt like a weight was lifting off her shoulders. She knew this would be killing him, but he was still giving her room to breathe, room to heal. 'I guess I should go today. I don't want to make this any more difficult.'

'Do you need a hand to move?' She could see the emotions on his face now. The pain she'd caused him bubbled beneath the surface. How could she do this to him?

'No. No, thanks. I'll make other arrangements.' She had to. She couldn't hurt him any more.

'Then let me say goodbye.' He picked up last nights discarded jeans from the floor and pulled them on. He grabbed a T-shirt from the cupboard and walked through to her bedroom. Through to where Zachary lay sleeping in his crib.

She watched as he bent over and stroked the side of Zachary's face, whispering to him for a few minutes. She had no idea what he was saying and she was glad, because her legs currently felt like jelly.

He turned to face her, striding briskly from the room but stopping just for a second beside her.

His dark-rimmed eyes caught hers. She wanted to tell him she loved him. She wanted to tell him that she ached for his touch. She wanted to tell him that she would never feel about anyone else the way she currently felt about him.

He hesitated, just for a second, as if trying to fathom if he should say the words circulating in his brain or not. Then he gave her a little smile. 'You were my One That Got Away, you know?'

'What?' His words confused her.

He moved closer. 'They say everyone has one. *The One That Got Away.* The one person that if you could turn back the clock and do something different for, you would. Anything that would have stopped them leaving. You were mine, Amy. And you always will be.'

His eyes met hers. 'Maybe this is right for us.' He glanced around him, his gaze sweeping over the apartment. 'There's something that I've wanted to do for a while— something I've been putting off. This might just give me the time to do that.' He looked thoughtful then reached over and squeezed her hand. 'Promise me you'll keep in touch.'

Her lips trembled. 'I promise,' she whispered as he kissed her cheek once more and walked out the door.

She stared down onto the San Francisco street and watched him walk briskly along the sidewalk. This was hard. Harder than she could ever have imagined.

But inside she knew it was right. She'd made a decision. Out there was the man she loved. She wanted to be with him with her whole heart.

She just needed to learn how to love herself first.

CHAPTER TEN

AMY drew a deep breath before climbing the stairs. She couldn't hide the tremble in her arm as she lifted her hand to ring the bell. It was a quiet, unassuming street, with trees lining the length of it, giving it an air of suburbia in the middle of the city. The gold plaque next to the door glistened in the sun. *Donna Kennedy, Counsellor.*

Normally she would have done this kind of thing by recommendation. Taking the word of a few reliable colleagues and friends. This time she'd made an appointment with the first counsellor she'd found in the *Yellow Pages* who would see her with a baby. She only hoped the warm friendly voice on the phone lived up to reputation she'd built in her head.

The door swung open. A small round woman with grey hair lifted Zachary straight out of her arms. 'Come in, come in.' She bustled Amy into a wooden-floored room that looked out over a wide garden filled with colourful flowers, pointing her in the direction of a comfortable leather armchair.

Everything about the place was friendly and inviting. The sunlit room was spacious enough to be comfortable but not sparse and clinical and looking like so many other office spaces. Amy could hear someone clattering around in the kitchen behind her, the smell of baking inviting her stomach to rumble. This was a home.

The woman settled herself in another chair, adjusting Zach in her arms as she chattered non-stop to him. Her smile lit up her face. 'It's been a long time since I got my hands on a baby.' She stuck her pudgy finger into Zach's little fist, waiting until his tiny fingers clenched hers.

Amy sank back into the chair. A pitcher of iced water and a couple of glasses sat on the small wooden table next to the chair. The windows to the back garden were open, letting the smell of cut grass and open blooms seep in through the air. She shifted in the chair. It was a little worn in patches, the leather thinning on the arms, but was obviously well used. Always a good sign.

She caught Donna's eyes on hers and instantly understood. This was a well-rehearsed routine. The easy, welcoming atmosphere. Taking the baby to allow her to relax, to focus on the reason she was here. She might look like a bustling grandmother, but this woman was wise.

A warm feeling swept over her. She'd come to the right place.

Donna gave Zach's head a little rub with her fingers, tracing them down his heavy eyelids—almost hypnotising him to sleep. Then, once she was satisfied with the outcome, she looked Amy straight in the eye. This woman was a professional through and through. 'So, Amy, tell me, how do you feel?'

No preamble. No 'explain why you are here'. Just straight to the point, 'how do you feel?'

Amy pressed her shoulders back into the armchair. Zach was quiet; he was sleeping. The sun was beating down on the grass outside and she could see birds pecking at the berries on the bushes next to the window. She took a deep breath. She could do this. This was easy. Everything about this felt right. But more importantly, for her, the time was right.

She looked Donna straight in the eye. 'I feel angry,' she said.

The plane circled a few times. The rain was torrential and was obviously affecting their ability to land. Time after time they swept over the darkening green rainforest as they waited for a suitable landing spot. From here, if Lincoln strained his eyes in the distance he could see the snaking Amazon, winding its way through the forest.

Home to hundreds of potential patients.

He'd successfully negotiated a variation in his contract, allowing him some extra unpaid leave from San Francisco to serve with the Amazon aid boat.

It hadn't been difficult. The hospital needed some good publicity right now, so supporting one of their best doctors on some aid missions had been an easy move for them. It helped that as the President's doctor he was still the darling of the media and could whip up some support for the people out here.

He'd managed to persuade a few colleagues at other hospitals to help out, assembling a team with a wide range of skills. Some of the best surgeons in the country were taking a few weeks out of their vacation time to come and do a series of operations on some seriously ill children. The planning had been a logistical nightmare, but at the end of the day these children would get what they needed. And the people of the world would get to see their plight as a film crew had decided to tag along for the ride.

Normally Lincoln would have avoided filming at all costs but he knew that interest in him would soon wane so he wanted to make the most of the opportunity to show the world the healthcare needs in the Amazon. It might even attract a few more willing docs to join the service on a regular basis.

The staff at San Francisco had been great, helping him with fundraising activities and praising his humanitarian efforts.

But Lincoln wasn't really going to help the people of the Amazon. That had always been at the heart of his work, and had been the only reason he'd volunteered in the first place.

But this time was different. This time he was doing it for himself.

'Linc, it's your weekly call!'

Linc looked up from where he was finishing with the latest addition to their baby clinic. Alice, one of Linc and Amy's old colleagues on the boat, was brandishing the satellite phone and waving it at him furiously. He placed the newborn back in the cot and moved towards their communication room—probably the hottest room on the boat.

As usual the line was crackly. 'Hey, it's Linc,' he said as he flopped down into the nearest seat.

'Hi, Linc, how are you doing?' He leaned backwards in his chair. The weekly telephone calls from Amy had started a month after he'd started back on the boat, a few days after he'd received her letter telling him she was doing well.

'How's Zach?' He always asked about Zach first. He couldn't believe how much he missed the little guy.

'Zach's good. He was at the clinic last week. They thought he might be developing a bit of a squint, so they've referred him to an ophthalmologist.'

'Who?' The words caught his attention instantly and he leaned forward in the chair. It didn't matter that he was on the other side of the world. He wanted to know what was happening to Zach.

'Some woman called Fern Price. She specialises in kids and is supposed to be very good.'

He scribbled her name on a bit of loose paper he had in his pocket—he'd check up on her later.

'How's Alice's hair holding up?'

Lincoln laughed. Alice moaned about the state of her hair from the moment she got up until the moment she went back to bed. Lincoln leaned back in his chair and raised his voice. 'Be thankful you're on the other side of the planet, Amy.' He wrinkled his nose. 'Though looking at how frizzy Alice's hair is, I'm surprised you can't see it from there.'

'What?' The shriek came from the other room. 'I'll get you for that, Lincoln Adams.'

Lincoln smiled. That's why he was here. This was what he needed. Friendship. Companionship and a lot of distractions.

'I saw you on TV again last night.'

'What?'

'On TV. The reporters love you.'

'As long as they bring more funding I don't care. A few more recruits would be nice too.'

'I wish I was there.' Her voice sounded wistful.

He felt a tingle run down his spine. 'I wish you were here too. but we both know an Amazon aid boat isn't the right place for Zach.'

He heard her take a deep breath. 'Are you coming back soon?'

He looked around at the battered boat, with its depleted medical supplies and too few staff.

'No,' he said firmly. 'I've still got work to do here.'

'I miss you, Linc. We miss you.' She hesitated a little. 'And I've got a surprise for you when you come back.'

'Really? What is it?'

'I've applied for a new job.'

'Really? Where?'

'In San Francisco.'

His heart stopped. She hadn't wanted to stay in San Francisco. She'd wanted to stay in Santa Maria and bring her child up in a community rather than a city. The hugeness of the step wasn't lost on him. The line crackled, a sure sign it was about to disconnect.

'Linc, speak to you next week,' he could hear her shouting.

'Sure,' he said as the line fizzled and died.

He stared at the satellite phone as the little red light flickered the cut-out.

'I've got a surprise for you too,' he whispered.

The weekly calls were hard—on both of them. But at least it was a starting point. Part of him wanted to go home right now, and part of him wanted to stay here in the Amazon, where he could hold on to his heart.

He pulled his wallet from his back pocket and found the dog-eared photo he was looking for. Zach, smiling and chewing on a toy. He smiled at it then peered closely at his eyes, looking for any sign of a squint. But there was nothing he could see. And what he really wanted to do right now was pull Zach onto his lap and look at him for himself.

He looked at the calendar. Three weeks. Another three weeks then he would head home. He'd tell her nearer the time. Until then his dreams would be haunted by a pale-skinned redhead.

'Linc, we need you!'

The voice stirred him from his thoughts as he saw people dashing about next door. Another emergency. Another life at stake.

Right now he was where he needed to be.

CHAPTER ELEVEN

THE bright lights were waiting for him at the airport—again.

Lincoln sighed. He'd just flown from Iquitos airport in Peru to Lima then Mexico City and on to San Francisco. He was exhausted. He'd been travelling for more than fifteen hours and all he wanted to do was collapse into bed.

He pasted a smile onto his face. In the last few months he'd gone from being the President's doctor to being the Amazon doctor and filmed for a US television series that was now beamed around the world. For some reason unknown to Linc, the people of the world seemed to love him. Television news crews followed his every move.

'Lincoln! Lincoln!'

A crowd of teenage girls were waiting at the arrivals gate for him, all wearing T-shirts adorned with his face and thrusting autograph books towards him. He swung his rucksack onto the floor—the rest of his luggage had gone missing at Lima airport, again. He smiled and posed for photos patiently. He could do this. It was all for a good cause.

An impatient TV reporter tapped him on the shoulder, flicking her dark hair and batting her eyelashes at him. 'Can you tell us, Dr Adams, are you going back to the Amazon?'

He'd just landed. He hadn't even had a chance to get his hands on an American hot dog yet and she wanted to know when he'd be going back.

He kept his smile carefully in place. 'I'm home to do some work at San Francisco's Children Hospital—where my regular day job is. I've got a list of surgeries that need to be scheduled for some kids in the Amazon, but I'll need to take a bit of time to try and organise that. A lot of the surgeons we require have very specialised fields and tight schedules so it could take a few months.'

The TV reporter flicked her hair again. 'Can't someone else do that for you?'

Lincoln shrugged his shoulders. 'Amazon Aid is trying to arrange a co-ordinator for me, but it has to be someone who understands the types of equipment and skills we require. It's a big job.' Despite his tiredness he shot her a beaming smile. 'I'm sure they'll find me someone soon, but in the meantime your viewers can donate to the charity or, if they've got a medical background, volunteer to help out on one of our missions.' He looked straight into the camera. He'd learned in the last few months that every piece of publicity helped. Applications for the Amazon aid boats had shot up since the television series had been screened. Some keen women had even tried to lie on their CVs about their qualifications—all in an attempt to get closer to him.

He had a whole pile of applications in his rucksack, along with some significant other paperwork that he'd had to come back to the States to sort out. It was amazing how things could change.

But more than that, something inside him had changed. Something deep inside. And whether he liked it or not, he'd Amy to thank for it. First Zach, and now another child with a pair of dark brown eyes, currently clouded by childhood cataracts, and a smile that could melt his heart. Another child pulling him in. With something he could cure. A kid whose parents had abandoned him on the boat, thinking his damaged eyes made him worthless. A kid he fully intended to bring home with him.

The reporter batted her eyelashes again. Did she have something in her eye? She was really beginning to annoy him.

She ran her hand up his arm, looking like a leopard about to pounce. 'So, Dr Adams, all work and no play makes Linc a dull boy. What do you plan on doing now you're home?'

The way she said his name grated. He felt as if a snake was currently crawling up his arm—and he'd seen enough of them recently.

His reply was curt and to the point. 'Sleep.' Interview over. He swung his backpack over his shoulder and headed towards the door.

But something caught his attention. A flash of a red jacket with the Amazon Aid sign, topped by a mane of red curls and a set of arms clutching a squirming toddler.

A hand caught his wrist. 'Lincoln. You're back. Great. Meet your new surgical co-ordinator.'

Brian Frew, the man behind the organisation of all the Amazon Aid expeditions, looked extremely pleased with himself. 'Lincoln, meet Amy. Amy, meet Lincoln.'

He froze. He'd never seen her wearing red before. It wasn't a colour normally associated with women with red hair. But Amy looked stunning. She gave him a wide smile. 'Told you I had a surprise for you.' She stretched her hand out towards him. 'Pleased to meet you, Dr Adams.'

His eyes fixed on Zach. Now approaching his first birthday, he was obviously developing well. He still had that lean look about him—common for babies born prematurely—and would probably never be a chunky toddler.

Amy had obviously been keeping hold of him in a vise-like grip and with one arm outstretched towards Lincoln Zach was currently making a break for freedom. Lincoln clasped Amy's outstretched hand and reached with the other for Zachary, who bounced over into his arms and started tugging at the leather thong around his neck.

'Hi, little guy. How are you?' he whispered. Green. His eyes were green now—just like his mother's. And they were straight. The patch he'd worn for a few months over one eye must have worked.

Amy cleared her throat. Brian was looking frantically from side to side, obviously wondering what was wrong. 'Can you give us a minute, please, Brian?' Amy's voice was strong and determined, with only the slightest waver. Brian nodded nervously and sloped off towards the door.

She stepped forward, into Lincoln's space, her face only inches from his.

'You're my co-ordinator?'

'I told you I'd applied for a new job in San Francisco. It almost seemed as if the job description was written for me. I decided it was time for me to show how much I wanted to be here. I left you a message on the satellite phone last week.'

He shook his head. 'I never got any messages. The satellite phone died last week, that's why I didn't phone to say I was on my way home.' She was right in front of him and he had Zachary in his arms. Ten long months he'd waited for this.

She smiled. A happy smile. A healthy smile. 'Well, now you're back in the country I intend to try and keep you here for a while.' There was a wicked glint in her eyes.

This was the Amy he had known. A confident woman, who knew what she wanted.

The implication was clear.

He took a deep breath. It almost felt as if his life were flashing before his eyes. Was he dreaming this? At some point on the plane he'd drifted off and his dream had definitely resembled this one. Could he still be sleeping on the plane?

No. His plane dream would never have included that obnoxious reporter. He looked at the green eyes in front of him. They were sparkling. And they were definitely there—this wasn't wishful thinking. There was only one thing he could ask her. 'How are you, Amy?'

She moved even closer, sliding one arm around behind Zach's squirming body and the other palm flat on Lincoln's chest. His eyes drifted downwards. Her chest was pressing towards him. Both sides of her chest.

She followed his gaze downwards and smiled. 'I guess I should have said I had two surprises for you. I took the steps I needed to. I figured since you already didn't object to scar tissue, you could handle a little more. I'm healed. I'm whole.' She lifted her head, staring directly into his eyes. 'I have a wonderful counsellor—I'd like you to meet her. And I am now "officially"...' she gave a little curtsey '...five years cancer-free.'

He took a deep breath, his heart pounding in his chest. 'That's great news. I'm happy for you. But what does this mean for us?'

He watched her, waiting for her to speak. Hoping and praying she'd say the words he was looking for.

'I have some unfinished business.'

Not what he'd expected. It sounded so formal. But, then, she was Miss Unpredictable. Could he really live a life like this?

'Business? With me?' He raised his eyebrow at her.

She nodded. Her hand moved from his chest, around his waist and down to his behind. 'I've done everything I can. I've taken care of what I can. Physically, mentally, emotionally, I'm ready, Linc. I'm ready to start again. And I'm hoping you are too.' Her eyes held his. Her lips were trembling. Was she about to cry?

'I just need to ask you one question.'

'What's that?'

'Can you take me as I am? Can you live with only ever having one child? Can you live with a woman who can't give you any children? Are you ready to give me another chance? Because I can promise you I'll never hurt you again. You've given me a lot of time to think about things. Can you give me a chance again?'

He smiled. Little did she know what he held in his bag. The future he had already planned. He kissed her forehead, then her eyelids, then her cheeks. 'I think I can manage that,' he whispered. 'And I've got a little surprise for you too—one I'll tell you about later.'

She took a deep breath. 'Good.' She leaned in and wrapped her arms around his neck, with Zach between them. 'Well, in that case, I've come to get my One That Got Away.' The tears were gleaming in her eyes. 'Because it was always you, Linc.'

And this time the tears were in his eyes too.

* * * * *

Mills & Boon® Hardback

May 2012

ROMANCE

A Vow of Obligation	Lynne Graham
Defying Drakon	Carole Mortimer
Playing the Greek's Game	Sharon Kendrick
One Night in Paradise	Maisey Yates
His Majesty's Mistake	Jane Porter
Duty and the Beast	Trish Morey
The Darkest of Secrets	Kate Hewitt
Behind the Castello Doors	Chantelle Shaw
The Morning After The Wedding Before	Anne Oliver
Never Stay Past Midnight	Mira Lyn Kelly
Valtieri's Bride	Caroline Anderson
Taming the Lost Prince	Raye Morgan
The Nanny Who Kissed Her Boss	Barbara McMahon
Falling for Mr Mysterious	Barbara Hannay
One Day to Find a Husband	Shirley Jump
The Last Woman He'd Ever Date	Liz Fielding
Sydney Harbour Hospital: Lexi's Secret	Melanie Milburne
West Wing to Maternity Wing!	Scarlet Wilson

HISTORICAL

Lady Priscilla's Shameful Secret	Christine Merrill
Rake with a Frozen Heart	Marguerite Kaye
Miss Cameron's Fall from Grace	Helen Dickson
Society's Most Scandalous Rake	Isabelle Goddard

MEDICAL

Diamond Ring for the Ice Queen	Lucy Clark
No.1 Dad in Texas	Dianne Drake
The Dangers of Dating Your Boss	Sue MacKay
The Doctor, His Daughter and Me	Leonie Knight

Mills & Boon® Large Print

May 2012

ROMANCE

The Man Who Risked It All	Michelle Reid
The Sheikh's Undoing	Sharon Kendrick
The End of her Innocence	Sara Craven
The Talk of Hollywood	Carole Mortimer
Master of the Outback	Margaret Way
Their Miracle Twins	Nikki Logan
Runaway Bride	Barbara Hannay
We'll Always Have Paris	Jessica Hart

HISTORICAL

The Lady Confesses	Carole Mortimer
The Dangerous Lord Darrington	Sarah Mallory
The Unconventional Maiden	June Francis
Her Battle-Scarred Knight	Meriel Fuller

MEDICAL

The Child Who Rescued Christmas	Jessica Matthews
Firefighter With A Frozen Heart	Dianne Drake
Mistletoe, Midwife...Miracle Baby	Anne Fraser
How to Save a Marriage in a Million	Leonie Knight
Swallowbrook's Winter Bride	Abigail Gordon
Dynamite Doc or Christmas Dad?	Marion Lennox

Mills & Boon® Hardback

June 2012

ROMANCE

A Secret Disgrace	Penny Jordan
The Dark Side of Desire	Julia James
The Forbidden Ferrara	Sarah Morgan
The Truth Behind his Touch	Cathy Williams
Enemies at the Altar	Melanie Milburne
A World She Doesn't Belong To	Natasha Tate
In Defiance of Duty	Caitlin Crews
In the Italian's Sights	Helen Brooks
Dare She Kiss & Tell?	Aimee Carson
Waking Up In The Wrong Bed	Natalie Anderson
Plain Jane in the Spotlight	Lucy Gordon
Battle for the Soldier's Heart	Cara Colter
It Started with a Crush...	Melissa McClone
The Navy Seal's Bride	Soraya Lane
My Greek Island Fling	Nina Harrington
A Girl Less Ordinary	Leah Ashton
Sydney Harbour Hospital: Bella's Wishlist	Emily Forbes
Celebrity in Braxton Falls	Judy Campbell

HISTORICAL

The Duchess Hunt	Elizabeth Beacon
Marriage of Mercy	Carla Kelly
Chained to the Barbarian	Carol Townend
My Fair Concubine	Jeannie Lin

MEDICAL

Doctor's Mile-High Fling	Tina Beckett
Hers For One Night Only?	Carol Marinelli
Unlocking the Surgeon's Heart	Jessica Matthews
Marriage Miracle in Swallowbrook	Abigail Gordon

Mills & Boon® Large Print

June 2012

ROMANCE

HISTORICAL

MEDICAL